Too Small for Basketball

Also by Kris Kenway

Precious Thing

Too Small
for Basketball

Kris Kenway

∫

SCEPTRE
Hodder & Stoughton

First published in 2001 by Hodder and Stoughton
A division of Hodder Headline
A Sceptre book

British Library C.I.P.
A CIP catalogue record for this title is available from the British Library

ISBN 0340 79271 X

Typeset by Palimpsest Book Production Limited,
Polmont, Stirlingshire
Printed and bound in Great Britain by
Mackays of Chatham plc,
Chatham, Kent

Hodder and Stoughton
A division of Hodder Headline
338 Euston Road
London NW1 3BH

Question: Hey Shaq! What was it like to be so tall as a teenager?

Shaquille: Some days it was great, some days it was a pain, just like any teenager goes through.

I.

QUEEN CRESS

I'm here to wreck her life. I know what people think about her, and it's those things that make me sick. Sicker now than before. You know her, too. Well, you've seen her. She's the face and body in a mid-range bikini, looking at you when you walk into Warehouse; she's wearing a white T-shirt and khakis in a big poster when you walk into The Gap; she's sitting with a group of too-healthy, all-American youths, outside a leafy college, for Ralph Lauren. She's the little girl with a secret that even she doesn't know. She's not on the news and you wouldn't recognise her on the street. But you know her.

Cress is only just out of her teens, and her fine white-blonde hair has thickened with age, but only darkened a little. Her green-brown eyes smile with kindness like they always have; they shine unnaturally, it's disturbing. She's tall, of course, and holds herself well. And many people tell her, throughout her day, as she chews her gum and drinks her herbal tea, that she's the greatest. They tell her that she's the queen. And maybe there's a part of her that likes that, that needs it, but it's hard to believe.

I push the driver's seat as far back as I can. It's still a squeeze. My flatmate's car wasn't built for me. I accelerate as I think about Peri's ultimatum, Peri's face

– our lives intertwined with each other in a way that even the sharpest knife couldn't separate.

I haven't seen Cress for a while. She's changing so fast. There's a calmness in her open face, her large eyes, wide mouth. You can see why she's a model. And her quirk is her cheekbones. They aren't amazingly angled like some models', they're just raised a little more than most people's, which gives her a girlishness, a look which matches her smiling temperament. I walk into the studio. I've never watched her with a photographer before. He has that kind of bad stubble men get when they can't grow a beard properly, an uneven rash across his face. His little inset eyes peer out at her. Perhaps he thinks some of her presence will rub off on him. Or that she'll just rub against him. He's in his forties, and people – including himself – only use his surname. He refers to himself in the third person. I sit in the corner and watch her look at him, into the beady lens and the beady eyes. I don't know which has less soul. It's close.

She looks left and right and up and down. She sits on white blocks against white backgrounds and all you can see is her – a suspended angel, today's doll, sitting in the corner of a converted warehouse in Brent Cross. She's wearing a silver sparkle vest, tight to her body, and matching knickers. Her naked legs and arms are exposed, her neck. I feel an awkward acid rise in my throat. I can't swallow but I can cringe, my embarrassment – or is it a feeling of helplessness? – making its physical appearance. A PA girl comes up to me, all ponytail and pretend-to-be-busy air about her. She asks me if I have a pass as the photographer is really

2

funny about strangers on his set. I tell her I have a pass. I don't know what a pass is. I finish the bottle of water I've had with me all day; it's warm now, and I remember that expression 'backwash' which we used when we were young. I look into the bottle and there are tiny particles – I don't know what of – floating around in the dregs. I pull out a magazine from my jacket, start reading it. I feel happier now, lost in the magazine, not looking around the room. My hands are shaking a little, and I think about my father, and what his face looked like as he told me the things which I would have given anything not to have known. And because he told me, I now have the power to screw up Cress's happy existence. But so does Peri. Perhaps it's a race between us. I finish with my magazine, take out a long credit card receipt from my wallet and start drawing on it. Another PA comes over to me, flicking her hair, wittering into a mobile phone about how 'Robson is a genius' and how 'essentially he's a sculptor with light, a poet.'

'*Fackin*' lovely,' Robson shouts to Cress and the shutter repeats like gunfire. I look up at the PA girl, who decides not to say anything to me. Are these people's lives worth less than the rest of ours? Yours are worth something; mine is worth something; Cressida's is worth everything. And I'm here to wreck her life.

The professional lights, recreating reality – only better – are switched off and the room loses the tension it had before. Now it's just a warehouse. Now it's just a space. I don't move anywhere. I watch the photographer go up and hug Cress and I can hear him say: 'Brilliant,

3

wonderful, so pleased.' She smiles a little awkwardly, but holds his hug. He's wearing a jacket even though we're inside, and knackered old jeans, black boots. She's wearing almost nothing. I feel sick again. I don't like this. *You keep repeating this because it isn't how you truly feel*, Mark's words echo. The photographer finally releases her and she walks off through a curtain and disappears. He slaps one of the sparks on the back as he leaves through another door. 'Have you ever seen legs . . . ?' His high voice trails off. The tough, gritty-looking spark gives him a raised eyebrow then nods unconvincingly, not enjoying this attempt at bonding. The photographer says, 'heh, heh,' like he has something to celebrate. I resist the urge to go up to him and pull one of those cables round his neck, sending a few volts into him. Although it might stimulate some more even facial hair.

He and the spark are gone now and my back is starting to ache from the uncomfortable seat. Thousands of tubes of moisturiser are scattered all around the studio. Cress must have held a million tubes during the afternoon, rubbed gallons of it into her arms, her legs, until her skin was saturated. I couldn't understand why they kept needing to change tubes. Now I notice there's different writing on each of them: Spanish, English, French, Japanese. They shoot the campaign for all the territories in one go. The PA comes back, this time with a helper.

'The shoot is over now,' she says, very primly. The other one looks at me, like she's gearing up to say something too.

4

'Can you leave please? We don't have any record of you being allowed here.'

Cress walks towards us and the two girls turn round and practically bow; it's so disgusting. I get up, although my back nearly gives way as I do. Cress puts her arms around me and gives me a hug. She's wearing a thick black skirt – the kind you could cross jungles in. She has on a grey top, with a jacket over it. She has no socks on, and there's a bag over her shoulder.

'Shall we go?' Cress says to me. 'I'm exhausted.'

'Sure.'

'What's on that?' she asks, looking at the receipt in my hand. 'Is that me you've drawn on there?'

I look at it, for the first time noticing that it was her.

'Can I keep it?' she asks.

'Are you mad?'

The two PAs are looking at us, trying to figure it all out: all the background.

'You two do look similar,' one says. The other nods.

'I'd like it.' Cress snatches the receipt out of my hand, ignoring them. She looks at it and smiles, puts it in her pocket. We walk to the car. I get in and unlock her side. The two PAs are in the doorway now, pretending to talk to someone who's just arrived, but they can't resist looking over at us in the car.

'Well, this is a surprise. Why'd you come down today? I thought you worked twenty-four hours a day,' she says. 'I haven't seen you for bloody ages. Everyone is always asking where you are. I thought you were

5

in a mood because of me doing this. Like you didn't approve.'

I shrug.

'Well, do you? Approve?'

'You can do what you like,' I say to her. She seems satisfied.

'You looked uncomfortable, watching me,' she says, laughing. 'You should come and see me dance sometime, you might like that. It's less trashy, it might come up to your expectations.' She pauses. 'You know I only do this for the money.'

I pull out of the industrial estate which was standing in for moisturiser heaven this afternoon, and onto the main road.

'I'm sorry, Marlow. I've had a crappy day. I'm sorry. It's great to see you. When you said you were coming to see me I thought someone must've died or something,' she says.

She lights a cigarette.

'No one's died, have they?' she asks, all concerned. I shake my head. 'Whose car is this?'

'My flatmate's. Lent it to me.'

'You want a fag?' she asks. When I don't answer she carries on puffing away.

'God, I always forget how quiet you are,' she says, waving to someone in the street.

'Who you waving at?' I ask.

'That person.'

'Who are they?'

'I don't know. They were waving at me.'

'Jesus.'

She sticks the radio on, there's a newsflash, a jocular man says that Nick Leeson has been arrested for ripping off Barings Bank for millions of pounds. He has bankrupted one of the oldest banks in the country. The DJ sounds very excited.

'Did you hear that, Marlow?'

'Of course I did. I'm sitting the same distance away as you are.'

'Do you care?'

'Not really.'

So she retunes the radio until it finds a dance station. I interrupt the track by quickly hitting a preset button. The radio zooms in on the strongest signal, a DJ is joking with his man in an aeroplane, talking about the traffic. The DJ talks right up to the split second before the lyric in the song kicks in. When the song ends it slips straight into a jingle, 'This *is* ninety-five point eight . . .'

'Keep it Capital,' I say, looking at her.

'Looking forward to seeing my flat?' she asks.

'Oh yeah.'

I'm sorry, Cress. I'm sorry for what I have to say.

'Wow, we just had a conversation then, Marlow. While we're talking, yeah, what has—'

I turn the song right up so I can't hear her and she can't hear me. Aretha Franklin belts it out. Cress turns the volume down a bit, mouths 'idiot' at me. Then she just jigs around in her seat a little. And we keep on driving. My mind has wandered off from its mission. I enjoyed the exchange and have, for a moment, forgotten why I'm here. I got here before Peri did, that's the first thing. And I'll do less damage, that's the second. I don't disapprove

7

of what Cress is doing at all, and I'm sure she sells more sunglasses, soap and clothes for these companies. Loving her just makes me the same as everyone else. But when acres of her skin are displayed on the page of a French beauty magazine – those ones that always smell so good – in an advert for bottled water, it doesn't do for me what the advertisers were hoping. It makes me gag. Honestly. It does.

Well, she's not your sister.

4'6"

2.

THE RAPE OF THE LOCK

Blurred Jesus. Look at him, he's all blurred and every-thing, and you can't make out his face because the paper is yellow and old. He's been looking down at me from up there for yonks. I think he's been there forever. The picture was a birthday present, because they couldn't find me a Sherman tank. The picture was my second great granny's, the one who went funny and said she was married to St Francis. But the air and the damp and everything got to the picture before me. I keep asking Mum if I can take Jesus down off my wall and put him somewhere and she always says, 'Jesus is bloody well staying right there.' So he stays right there, next to a picture of the singer with all the hair and the guitar which is shaped like a 'V'.

Sausage has pictures of ponies in her room. Sausage has blonde hair and a voice which comes through her nose like she has a cold. She calls me *Barlow*. She likes to dress up in stupid clothes. Mum took her to a Christingle service at Christmas last year because she was hoping Sausage would like God more than I do. She thought this was the *bloody* way to get Sausage into it. I'm not allowed to swear. Mum thought those oranges with the jelly tots on sticks stuck in them, all that Christingle stuff, would do it. Mum was pretty angry I wouldn't go. She said she wanted to be seen with at least one of her children. She shouted all about it for a while. But there's no way I'm going to church. I'm nearly nine, and church is boring. I don't believe in God, and I reckon the Cyclops could easily have Him in a fight.

'If you think the Cyclops could beat God, then you believe God exists,' Mum always says.

Mum dragged Sausage away from Janey's party to go to the Christingle. Sausage had her fancy dress party clothes on: high heels, a dress too long for her, one of those pink fluffy feather things that looks like a scarf or a snake, and tons of make-up. Well, during the car journey Mum tried to drive while wiping Sausage's face but ended up just smudging the lipstick everywhere so she was like a clown. That's what Sausage looked like. She's five. Her real name is Cress, which is short for something. And while Mum was trying to drive and wipe the lipstick off Sausage's face, she scraped along a car which was parked by the church. It belonged to someone she knew. Their mirror got ripped right off by our car and made a loud noise and Mum shouted and Sausage screamed and everyone cried. Once they were in there, Sausage had to go up to the front of the church with all the other kids, holding their oranges and candles, while the mothers looked on and everyone sang those hymns about how God is great and we're all rubbish. Well, when Sausage went up there she really took her time, made sure everyone could see her. Then she did a little dance, and bowed. She was the biggest hit of the service. Everyone went, 'Ahhh,' and thought she was really sweet. She knew what she was doing, I reckon.

She took all the praise afterwards, then refused to talk to anyone on the way home, nose in the air. Mum said Sausage would probably be an actress.

Today we went to get my birthday present. The three of us went: me, Mum and Sausage. My Dad said I should have something special because nine is important. So I said a lizard would be brill. They didn't look too happy about that. Dad couldn't come – he works all the time, and doesn't like shopping. He likes to work on his old car at the weekend, taking it apart. It was so busy at the Paradise Arcade today – everyone goes there because it's great. Mum didn't want to go, she was on the phone to Dad saying, 'I can't do it'. She really hates lizards. Last time at the arcade I put a slinky on an escalator and everyone stopped to watch, but there wasn't enough room this time. I got bumped into all the time and Sausage thought it would be ace to walk along with her eyes closed, so she kept falling over. I was in charge of her. It's always more fun if we take Sausage. But the thing was, we couldn't find any shops selling lizards no matter where we looked.

'Can you read that, Marlow?' Mum said, pointing up to a banner.

I read it. '*Welcome to the greatest shopping experience in the south-east.*'

'A is for apple,' Sausage said to herself, as we walked along. 'B is for b*aa*na.'

'Banana,' I said. She didn't take any notice.

'C is for . . .' she couldn't think of nothing. 'C is for . . .'

13

'Turkey,' I said.

After a bit I got well bored, and wished I'd stayed over at Danny's instead – he's found some of those magazines for grown-ups down by the lay-by. He wouldn't let me see them. Then Mum saw something she liked in a shop but she didn't want to try it on. So I said I would look after Sausage while she did. She sort of frowned for a bit then said okay. Off she went into the trying-on room. Sausage got bored after a minute and dragged me into the toy bit, next to the clothes. She never really talks much. Last year she didn't talk at all for a bit, then she started again. I'm the one always chatting, Mum says. I'm always in trouble for asking questions, but Dad says that's the only way you learn and he thinks it's good. There's so much stuff to talk about. Sausage picked up a big plastic necklace which was painted gold. It could have had an anchor on the end, it was so thick. Really old women with orange faces who smell of cigarettes and are about forty wear them! Sausage put it on and tried to walk out of the shop. I managed to stop her, but she wouldn't take the necklace off. So I asked how much it was and it turned out to be two quid, fifty. So I paid the whole lot with all my money and kept the receipt so I could get the money off Mum or smash Sausage's piggy bank later. I walked her back to the changing rooms and waited for Mum to come out. Well, Sausage and me were standing there and I was just thinking to myself a bit, about how I really wanted to get my lizard today. I was looking forward to it.

Then this alarm went off – it wasn't the normal alarm for the shop, it was really loud, and ringing out across the whole of the arcade and it started to echo, like when you're in Cheddar Gorge. I looked out through the glass front of the shop listening to this big, huge siren. Sausage and I sort of got dragged by the sound towards the door. I was holding her sticky little hand. People across the arcade were stopping what they were doing: walking, talking, eating. I couldn't believe what happened next: all the doors locked really quickly. Some people nearly got stuck in them. No one could get out. It was well scary. Sausage pulled her hood up with one hand and put her other hand over one of her ears. She looked like Little Red Riding Hood. We were still near the entrance to the shop, Sausage and me. Up and down the arcade people were standing dead still for no reason, they looked like Mr Freeze had zapped them. The only people who hadn't been zapped were two policemen who were running really fast, and everyone was getting out of their way. One of them shouted into his radio as he ran.

The alarm kept ringing.

Soon Sausage had a bloody great lollipop in her gob – I don't know where that came from. I could hear Mum's voice asking if they had seen an eight-year-old boy and a five-year-old girl anywhere. She was shouting really loud. I thought she was going a bit mad. I turned round and she saw us. She ran towards us, picked Sausage up. She was crying and asking herself why she was so stupid. She kept saying: 'How could I be so stupid,' a billion times. On and on. She shouted at me for wandering off and she was really red in the face. So Sausage started crying and then Mum was crying even more which I didn't like. I said 'don't cry' to her, but she kept on crying. I kept telling her to stop but she wouldn't. She had Sausage in her arms. Then I started crying but I didn't know why. I kept telling Mum to stop. I've never seen her cry before. She put her hand out for me but I wouldn't move because I wanted her to be normal.

'Not now, Marlow,' she said, really angry. So I held her hand but she walked too fast for me and I kept tripping up. She was carrying Sausage. We left the arcade really quickly. Mum didn't say anything on the way back. I felt sick when we got home. When Dad came back Mum cried again. He was hugging her a lot which made her better. I didn't want to watch her cry any more so I went upstairs. I didn't know grown-ups cried.

When I wake up I tell Mum she owes me five quid for that stupid necklace that Sausage got, and she pays it. Then I ask her, were there burglars at the arcade yesterday? Mum tells Sausage and me the reason the doors all closed quickly was probably a malfunction. Sausage asks what a 'muntion' was because she can't bloody say hardly any long words. Mum says it means broken. I go into my bedroom, but I can hear Mum on the phone in her room, across the landing. So I go and stand under Jesus, hanging on my wall by the door, so I can hear her better.

'No, she had two children with her . . .' Mum says to her friend. It's her new friend who says, *Oh la la!* the whole time because she thinks you have to do that once you've lived in a caravan in France for the summer. Mrs *Oh la la* was in the new shopping arcade, like us. Mum keeps talking,

'. . . They were looking at a window display . . . No, I

TOO SMALL FOR BASKETBALL

think she had one in her arms, and the other one in those child straps, you know . . .' Mum says. They tried to put those straps on me a couple of years ago but I went mad. They look like reins, like you're a reindeer.

'Well, she didn't feel any pressure on the reins so she looked round and there was nothing at the end of them. No, that's the thing, Heather, the end of the reins had been *cut*! Yes, well, that's why the security guard acted quickly . . . *exactly* . . . apparently there's one button that can lock all the exits . . . I know . . .' Mum listens for a bit, then she says quietly, 'You can't believe it, can you?'

Then I can't hear her at all. All I get is something about looking for this girl, something about walkie-talkies – I love walkie-talkies, maybe I'll get those instead of a lizard – and descriptions of the girl: long blonde hair, green eyes.

'Apparently one of the search groups found her. She was in a cubicle in the men's toilets. That's the thing, she'd only been missing for a few minutes . . . they'd shaved her head, changed her clothes . . .' I can hear Mum walking quickly around the kitchen while she talks.

'That poor woman,' Mum says. She says goodbye and hangs up the phone. Then she starts to cry. I go into the other room and tell her I know it wasn't the doors breaking that meant they all shut like that. Her face goes really white. She says, 'What do you mean, *you know*?'

I tell her I don't know why they would want that girl unless, I reckon, maybe she had some money on her.

Mum says, 'You know you see things on television about people in Britain adopting a child from Africa?'

I say, 'No.'

'Well,' she says, 'sometimes people would like a child and they might not be able to get one from Africa.'

'Why?'

She tells me not to think about it.

'Isn't it weird that Sausage looks like the girl they wanted?'

'Don't say that, Marlow, don't ever say that. You shouldn't have been listening to my conversation,' she says. She looks angry.

'No. I just . . . I just overheard . . .'

She turns round and wipes her eye; her hand is shaking. I get a chocolate bar from the drawer without asking. She turns around.

'Is eating all you do?' she says. 'Are you the biggest in your class yet?'

'Second biggest.'

She hugs me, but when I say something to her she doesn't answer; she's not listening. It doesn't feel like it normally does.

When I go to bed tonight I put up a big picture of the Cyclops right by Jesus in my room. Mum sees it but lets me keep it there. Cyclops and Jesus, right next to each other, having a scrap in my bedroom. I lie in bed and think about what it was like for that girl, with her head shaved like they did to the lion in *The Lion, the Witch and the Wardrobe*. Why would you do that? I wonder what she felt like, that little girl with two men she didn't know, in the Paradise Arcade.

3.

APPLE SAUCE

Two days later we go into town and finally I find a lizard in a big aquarium shop that has piranhas with jaws that stick out, like Granny Two's. They don't have any crickets there so we buy the one locust they do have and they say that when the new crickets come in the next day, they'll post them to me. They send them in the post! We put the locust in a cold box with two hot water bottles. The lizard is in a shoe-box with some holes in it, and it's wrapped in a blanket and stuck down on the floor of the passenger seat with the blower heater on full blast. I've set the tank up for the lizard already, but we still have to drive fast to get them back home quickly, like when an ambulance is in a hurry. Our two patients are a lizard and a locust. The policeman that stops Mum leans into the car and asks her why she's going so fast. Sausage rubs her lolly against the policeman's face as he looks in the car. My sister doesn't care. Mum tells him about the lizard and the locust and he thinks that's funny and lets us go. We could have been in prison for ever! We get back and stick her in the tank, and I decide to call her Lizzer. Then we put the locust in there. I watch her, but she doesn't move for three hours. Neither does the locust. So I watch a film on telly.

The next day I have to go to school but I'm thinking

about Lizzer all day. I tell everyone I've got a lizard and no one believes me. All my friends come round in the evening – there's ten of them! They think she's great and then all their mums want to come in and see her as well. They say to my mum, 'I think you're amazing.' I don't know why *she's* amazing. When I say it's a Mexican Oala, which I totally made up, any people at school who didn't reckon I really had a lizard suddenly believe me for defo.

Later on, after everyone has gone, I hear something from the corner of the room. When I look into the tank Lizzer has the locust in her gob. She's chewing it and the locust's feet are going mad. I watch her for hours after that. But after she's eaten the locust she goes to sleep. Like Dad does. I sit and watch her though, in case she does anything new.

I've got a headache now. The special light bulb, which is like the sun, is very strong in her tank and it's making my head hurt. All through the night I can hear this digging noise and when I wake up she's rearranged the whole tank and dug herself a hole under a piece of bark to sleep under. And her tail is shedding, which is called sloughing. I pick it out of the tank and stick it on my wall. Sausage asks me what it is and I tell her it's the lizard's tail and she cries, and isn't better until she's eaten a bowl of apple sauce. So I have two bananas cut up, with milk and sugar; a nut cereal bar and two After Eights. Sausage must have stopped thinking about the lizard's tail as she seems happy again. She has a pint of apple sauce a day, Mum says.

John Lennon dies today when I watch the television,

and everyone is very sad; on TV lots of people go and stand in a big park. I'm staying the weekend with Granny Two, who keeps interrupting the television and saying, 'Is this *Songs of Praise*?' when it's a cat food advert. And she keeps trying to tell me about her dead dog. I prefer Great Granny but she lives in one of those places, so we have to go and see her. Great Granny doesn't really talk; she just sits and eats Smarties. It takes her about a year to eat one; you can hear it rattling around for ages in her gob. I wonder if I could feed her a locust. Granny Two is different. She talks a lot. She goes on about how, in her day, sometime around those wars, you didn't have to pay a fare to take a dog on a bus. But you do nowadays. She told me she was walking old Crabtree in the park last week and he died on the spot.

'Tuesday last,' she says. 'Dropped dead. Had a heart attack. Best way to go. So I picked him up and when I got on the bus I said to the driver, "This dog is dead, I won't be paying its fare."'

We have ploughman's for lunch and I play cards with Grandpa who beats me. We have eclairs for pudding. I like being at their house but I miss my friends. We were all going to play football today – eight of us in the park, but I have to miss it. After football we usually have running races and I'm like Daley Thompson, then we have a scrap on the playing fields and I always win. Well, Colin Biggs always wins because he's massive, but I usually come second or third. I've always been one of the biggest. On the wall in our kitchen is a big poster of a giraffe, with different heights marked on it, all the way up to six and a half foot. There's a mark for me at

4'6" and one for Sausage at 3'8". I'm really big for my age. Sausage is normal.

In the afternoon Granny drives me back to my house. She stays for a cup of tea with Mum and tells her about the dog.

'I said, "This dog is *dead!* I will not being paying its fare."'

Mum smiles.

'If you were with a dead person and the two of you got onto a bus, would you have to pay for the dead person?' I ask.

'Well, I wouldn't. That's definite,' Granny says.

'I would,' I say.

'Misery guts,' Granny says, laughing.

'Misery *uguts*,' Sausage says. She's trying to eat a chicken drumstick but it's too big to get in in one piece so she opens her mouth really wide, closes her eyes and tries to stuff it in. She has a jaw like those snakes that can eat an elephant. Mum tells her to take little bites but she keeps on trying. Next time I look, it has gone.

'Tell you what, for your birthday next year, maybe we could buy your lizard a companion. You should come over to Upton, there's a great shop there. They have iguanas. It's much nicer than that arcade.'

'It made me frightened,' Sausage says.

'Where's Doyle?' Granny says. 'It's nearly eight o'clock.'

'Working as usual,' Mum says. 'He never stops.'

'How's the newspaper?'

'*It's* fine. But he and Don are working all day, all night, all weekend. Doyle looks worn-out the whole time.'

'It's terrible, isn't it?' Granny says and me and Sausage

nod like we agree. Sausage has ketchup all over her chops. Granny Two asks after Granny One. Granny One lives in London and we don't see her very often. She has a busy life since Grandpa died. She likes to dance on big ships which cruise for three weeks and leave from Southampton. I leave the table and go into my room. There's a box of crickets waiting there. The crickets are chirping really loudly but are much uglier than the locust. I miss that locust. Lizzer goes mental when I throw in five crickets, and she races around the tank biting them, and they hop and sing, and she jumps and skids and eats four of them. The fifth one chirps all night and keeps me awake but I suppose it was really happy it was alive. In the morning, Lizzer eats it.

On the first day of the holidays Mum takes me and Sausage to the cinema to watch *Xanadu*, which is now Sausage's favourite film. I like *Xanadu*, it's got roller skates in it, but I can't stop thinking about going in an aeroplane tomorrow. Mum says it's cheaper to go on holiday at Easter and there aren't so many people around. I go up on the flight deck on the way there while Dad snores. It's my first time abroad and on the first night we go out and I have a T-bone steak and a banana split. The air feels soft here. The next day I buy a T-shirt with my name on it and an ace dinghy that I'll use on the sea. I have a hot dog for lunch. On the second day we wait for the bus for ages so we end up sharing a taxi with two nice old ladies who only speak Portuguese.

When we wake up the next morning we can't find

23

Sausage anywhere, even though the front door was locked all night. We run around the apartment, looking for her everywhere. Mum is calling out her name. We check the front door and it's unlocked. Mum starts getting very scared and Dad is not around. He's always off by himself having walks. And sometimes when we're out we'll pass him, sitting on a rock, looking out to sea. I tell Mum that Sausage will definitely be around somewhere but she doesn't hear me. Mum shouts her name out really loud. She starts crying again. I don't like it. We go outside and find Sausage walking towards us, eating a lollipop. Mum picks her up, asks where she got the lollipop from, how she got out of the house. Sausage doesn't say anything. Mum finds her keys in Sausage's pocket, and some money she left on the table the night before. Sausage holds the lollipop up.

'Raspberry,' she says, and because of the sun her hair is now really fair, the same colour as the blurred Jesus on my wall. Then the doorbell goes and a kid about my age is standing there. He asks, in really weird English, if any of us want to buy any more of his lollipops. He holds his hands out, they're crammed full of them. Mum is still really upset so I go into my room and lie on my bed and close my eyes. A few hours later Mum comes in.

'Marlow, you've been in here for fifteen minutes. What's the matter?'

'Nothing.'

'Come on,' she says. So I get up. We go and have lunch to celebrate Sausage not being dead. When Mum tells Dad what happened he doesn't really say anything. He reads his book about Peter Sellers. Mum is really sad all day. I have another banana split with some green stuff in it which is drink, and all afternoon I have a headache and I'm not allowed out in my dinghy. I sunbathe for a while but that's boring so I go into my room and sit there for a while and try to look at a magazine I bought which is all in Portuguese, and however hard I try I *cannot* understand it. Sausage is in the next room so I go up to the door and look through the crack, and can see her hiding lollipops under her pillow like she's a criminal. Which she probably is. The rest of the holiday isn't so good. Mum is ill on one day and doesn't get out of bed. On the last day I get stung by something and my face goes all red and big. Luckily it goes down before school starts again.

On the first day back everyone is talking about their holidays. And that I'm now captain of the swimming team. I like going away but I miss my friends. I wish they could all come too. Danny has a big party on the first weekend back at his house. There are fifteen of us, all our best friends. And some girls come along too. After we've eaten our spaghetti we all go and scrap on the grass outside and the girls sit inside and they just talk. I'm not sure what they talk about.

4'9"

4.

TOO SMALL FOR BASKETBALL

I'm smaller than everyone. In every way I'm smaller than everyone I know. I'm so small I'm barely even there. Everyone here towers over me like giants. I've only grown three inches in four years.

I was ill last week. I never used to get ill. So I didn't start when everyone else did. I am a week behind. Behind everyone.

When I was about nine I left my old school because I was clever, or because I wouldn't bloody go to Sunday School – I can't remember. So I came to a new one, and left all my friends behind. The new one was okay, I went there for three years, and I got to do a lot of swimming which was cool. The people were all right, and in the evenings I could come back and see my real friends from home. Now I've moved schools again. You have to be thirteen to start this one. And I'm thirteen.

Last night we still weren't sure if I'd be okay to go. I helped clear the table after we had eaten, and then sat and read some comics. Cress wandered about the house, putting music on in every room. She put on a woman called Aretha Franklin really loudly and she sang along although she didn't know any of the words. Some of her friends came round and there was a lot of noise going on. She and the younger girl, Lucy, both giggled a lot and ran around the house singing and then went into her bedroom where they probably plotted to take over the world. The older sister came into the kitchen.

'What're you reading?' she asked.

'*Judge Dredd.*'

'I like *2000 AD.*'

'Really?'

'Yeah,' she nodded. 'What school do you go to?'

'I'm starting a new one tomorrow,' I said.

'Me too,' she said. 'I'm Peri.'

She stood with her arms folded in front of her and talked away. When I asked her if she wanted to sit down, she said she was fine. When I got up to get us a drink she moved for me to pass, even though there was loads of room. She did the same when Mum came into the kitchen: whenever anyone came close to her she would move aside quickly, her arms crossed tightly.

'Why don't you go and see Cress?' Mum said to Peri.

'I think she and Lucy are busy,' Peri said.

'Well, Marlow has homework to do. I'm sure Cress would like you to join in.'

'What homework does he have if he hasn't started yet?' Peri said. Mum shrugged and left the room. Peri and I kept talking. She was pretty and her eyes were nice. Her mum came and picked up her and Lucy and both mums talked at the door for a while, occasionally looking back at us. I told Peri good luck with her new school. When they left, my mum asked what we talked about and I said just comics.

'Anything else?' she asked.

'No, just comics,' I said.

Monday morning. A lot must have happened in that first week I was away. It feels like I don't know anyone. And they all seem to have grown over the summer holidays. They all talk differently; the way I talk seems really stupid. They're all talking about Live Aid. I like Iron Maiden. Different groups have formed already and people are calling each other by their first names, instead of their nicknames, or last names or *fuckhead*. I start to miss my last name and *fuckhead*. And the older boys, well, the ones two years up from us, I watch them as we sit in assembly. They look like proud lions, smelling of aftershave, with big gold rings on their fingers. I look the rings up in the Argos catalogue; some of them cost a fortune. And some of those boys wear slip-on shoes to school and some of those shoes have sort of little tassels on them where the laces would have been. And no one really talks to me, but then it *is* a long time since I saw a lot of them. Over the holidays I mostly saw my friends at home. And my lizards, they take up a lot of time. The oldest one, Lizzer, hasn't been well so I've been looking after her. And Peri, well I only met her last night but she's cool and lush. At my last school I was friends with lots of people. In the week I've been away, my friends have got to know all the new people really quickly; now they're friends with all the ones who came in from different schools.

The bell goes for lunch. I walk to the canteen, around the big athletics field in front of the main school block which looks scary. It looks old-fashioned and grand. I hate that. I like modern things. There are oil paintings of the old headmasters on the walls. They look stiff and stern and cruel. I sit down to eat lunch at a table. I sit there and wait as my friends come in. I keep looking up, trying to get their attention. They're at the hatch, getting their trays of food. It's like one of those prisons. One by one they all walk past me. I call out to them, but they go and sit at a table opposite. A nice sixth former comes over to me and asks if I want to sit with them instead of sitting by myself. I can see some of my old friends at a table across from me looking over. I pick up my tray and walk over to one of the sixth form tables. The boy tells me to sit by this girl, a sixth form girl, who has perfume on and is wearing make-up and lipstick, even though she isn't supposed to, I reckon. I sit by her and then this other boy tells me I have to kiss her. The girl laughs and says, 'Anthony, shut up.' But Anthony keeps on saying it.

I don't know what to do and then I realise all the tables are looking at me. I look back down at my food and keep eating. The food tastes and feels like something weird. I'm aware of every mouthful; it takes so long to chew, so long to swallow. I'm not used to people watching me; I like to just go by and not make a fuss. I don't like this; I don't know what to do. No one ever picked me out before. All the boys here look like they must shave all the time. I can feel my face burning red and I'm too scared to look up.

Then this boy Anthony says that if I didn't kiss her I'd have to run some laps. I don't know what those are, but they sound tiring. Then someone on the table says it's running around the football pitch. I look back down at my food and I can feel my eyes get all watery for no reason. Shit. My eyes feel like they're bulging. And I think about yesterday afternoon when I watched *Arthur* on TV with Cress and I was excited about seeing everyone again. And Peri came over and everything was so great, like it normally is.

I look up at the girl sitting by me who now looks scared and all of a sudden she smiles a little, and then she snaps at Anthony: 'Leave him alone.' I pick up my tray and shuffle to the end of the table. I stand up, and as I walk back, I feel my feet hit something and I start to fall. I look down and see Anthony's feet entangled with mine. The tray falls and the plate goes *smash!* on the floor and the forks and everything go *tinkle*, and the mince and the potato goes *splat!* And then I fall into it all. Everyone is laughing and I pick myself up just as a teacher walks in. He tells me to go and clean myself up. He seems angry with me. When I stand back up, everyone is still looking at me except the table of all my friends. They're looking down, eating their meals. I walk up to the table, 'Any of you coming back for a kick about?' I ask, just like normal. There's mince on my shirt, potato all down my arm. I can feel the warm food on my face, on my cheek. There's a sort of mumble from a couple of people but no one actually looks back at me. Later on I'll look back at that as a one-off incident. That was just first-day-back stuff. First-day-at-a-new-school stuff. It wasn't the same as what was on its way.

I walk back to the classroom, where there's no one around. I get out my lizard file and look up 'lizard diseases' again, although I've looked at the pages a million times. And those pages are four or five years old. I try to figure out what's wrong with Lizzer. I sit in the classroom by myself and look out through the window. It's another forty minutes until the next lesson starts and I can see the other boys walk out of lunch and wander around together in packs. They really stretch the days out here. It's a long time until seven p.m., when I can go home. I try to pronounce the different lizard diseases in Latin to myself.

When the bell goes for the end of the day, I walk down to where all the mothers are picking their children up. Well, they aren't children, apart from me. As I walk to the car I can see Cress sitting in the front seat, wearing a jacket too big for her and her hair all permed and disgusting. There are a million brown leather bracelets on her wrists. She's got lipstick on, and is listening to a Walkman. I get in the back of the car.

'How was your day?' Mum asks me.

'All right really,' I say.

'Just all right?'

'Yeah.'

'How was Danny and everyone? It must've been nice to see them again.'

I don't say anything.

'It's grand, this school, isn't it?' Mum liked the school from the minute she saw it. She liked the grounds and the buildings; she didn't see the people. She liked it because she'd like to live here, or have a holiday here. She didn't see the headmasters' pictures, the teachers, the tension, the people.

34

Cress doesn't even look round for the first half of the journey she's so engrossed in her Walkman. She's singing. 'Take on me, take me on . . .' Finally she does look round and she smiles at me and I tell her that her lipstick and her hair and A-ha are bloody stupid and she seems really pleased. Sometimes, if Mum is annoyed or really happy or in a hurry she gets her name wrong and it comes out, 'Oh, Sauscressie, er, Cress darling, hurry up!' Cress doesn't answer to anything but her name, and often she doesn't even answer to that.

I get ready to go out to the Roller Disco. We pick Marty up on the way. Marty is older than me and is my friend from the summer holidays. He's wearing a yellow cardigan and dark trousers with tiny flecks of bright colours in them. They look ace. And he has white slip-on shoes and fluorescent green socks. Marty has cool coloured tape on his roller skates, which are the same as what ice hockey people use, but you can put roller skates on the bottom instead. The Roller Disco is in the leisure centre and they're still packing away badminton nets when we get there. Mum doesn't like us out late so we always get there really early, even though it hasn't started, so she can say we had our two hours. We put on our boots and start skating around in circles. Then it really starts and the music comes on and we do that for two hours and then Mum, who waited outside and in the café, comes to pick us up. I'm quite tall with roller skates on. Just before we left I met a nice girl, who was about sixteen, called Hore. Marty said he didn't like her and she had a real reputation. She didn't seem that good a skater, if you ask me.

*   *   *

35

Two days later I'm at home and I'm sitting eating a sandwich and Mum asks me what's in my hair. I tell her it's this funny thing where people put butter in other people's hair. She asks me why I was putting butter in anyone's hair and I tell her that I wasn't. So she says: 'Right, so they just put it in your hair, then?' And I just finish my sandwich. Cress has also just started a new school but she's enjoying it. She's always coming home with some piece of material that she wants to turn into something. She starts to make something really complicated but usually gets bored of it and finally it ends up as a shawl. She has about a million shawls which started out as being something else, but after all that cutting, sewing, changing of mind and undoing, it's all they're any good for.

At the weekend Mum asks if any schoolfriends will be coming over. I tell her I don't really see those people any more.

'But they're still in your class, though?'

'Yes.'

'Why don't you see them, then?'

'I just don't.'

'You shouldn't just hang around with Marty. I know he's nice, but . . .'

I spend the afternoon putting different tape on my roller skates. When we go skating again Marty says they look ace and the girl called Hore throws some Coke over him as he says hello to her. Apparently that's Marty's name for her; it's not her real name. Marty is wearing tight black jeans and has had his hair cut in a flat top, which is cool and I want to get that done. They have a special comb with one of those bubbles in water to check it's level.

I go into lessons all day, sit there, and then at lunchtime I walk off into the town, sit on a bench somewhere, and read a magazine about radio-controlled cars or sometimes *Kerrang!* which is my new favourite magazine. I'm totally into Iron Maiden and Nuclear Assault, and no one else is! No one that I know. I send in a letter every week, but I haven't got one printed yet. Then I go to games, which I hate – they do rugby and football here, but mostly rugby – then we have tea. But my favourite bit of the day is reading *Kerrang!* which I have to stop because a teacher says I'm not allowed out at lunch-time and also because they all said, 'Why is a poof reading a heavy metal magazine?'

Back at home Mum asks, 'How was your first month?'

'Okay,' I say, and then tell her I have some homework I have to do. I go upstairs. Cress comes into my room.

'Get out!'

'Can I see the lizard?' she asks.

'No.'

'Why?'

'Just get out.'

'Why're you so nasty?' she says, and leaves the room.

This one boy, a real dick, comes up to me after lunch one day and tries to talk to me. He acts as if we're the same. I look away as he comes and sits by me. Then he starts saying, 'So, which school did you come from?'

37

What a nerd. But it's the first question anyone has asked me since I've been here.

'The same one as all that lot,' I say, pointing to them.

'No.'

'Yeah.'

'They said they didn't know you.'

'To you?'

'No, they don't talk to me. But I heard.'

Maybe I'm like him. I wish Marty went to this school: he's nice and he's so cool. No one here has flat tops – their hair is all floppy at the sides. I think about what it's like standing there with jam and Marmite in my hair, saying, 'Pete, d'you want to come round this weekend?' after he's just splatted me. He just laughs and wanders off. If I said it when he was by himself he would shrug and say, 'Yeah, maybe.'

I don't understand why this is happening. Why is it me? Why isn't it that nerd?

I don't tell Marty about my school, I just listen to him talk about motocross, which he's really getting into. He always wears his leather bike trousers, even when he's not racing. But on top of the trousers there's still the cardigan, and most of the time the cardigan is yellow. Marty asks me how I got the bruise around my eyebrow and I tell him how playing football with boys two years older is pretty tough. I show him a picture of the rugby team.

'Fuckin' hell. You're half the size of that lot. What year are they in?'

'My year.'

Marty points to one of them sitting at the front, holding the ball, 'That one's neck is as wide as your shoulders. What do they feed posh wankers?' People in the photo, people who I used to be taller and bigger than, now tower over me. My face looks small; my eyes running away from my face, trying to hide; my hands are small; my legs are short and thin; my shoulders are narrow; my voice is high. I only noticed all these things this month. It's like my friend Reggie, from my old school. He says he only knew he looked different when he started a new school. He only noticed he was different then.

I'm smaller than them all.

The best parts are the evenings. Even though I don't get home until really late I try and go over and see Richie, who's another friend from before. I watch *First Blood* at his house most nights. Richie is so cool, even though he doesn't have any tape on his roller skates. He has those crap ones which are suede and plastic, like the ones Sausage has. Marty comes round and I put on my new yellow cardigan which he thinks is ace, and he has a new ski jacket which is green and pink and some new pink slip-on shoes which look cool. He says they aren't pink, they're salmon.

'I saw this girl the other day, skatin', and you could really see her nipples,' Marty says.

'Nipples like JCB starter buttons!' Richie says, to no one. He sits there like an excited monkey, waiting for something.

'I buys you chips, I shags you, what more d'you want?' Richie says. He changes his voice, so it sounds all strained, 'You've done a man's job, Deckard . . . too bad she won't live, but then, who does?'

'What?' Marty says, looking at Richie like he's mental. Marty asks me if I know what Richie is talking about. I don't really have a clue most of the time. It's just him. He watches a lot of films.

'It's *Blade Runner*,' Richie finally says.

People analyse stuff a lot when they get bigger. It's like the way people comment on me and the things they call Reggie because his family is from Jamaica. Richie is quite tall – I only noticed that recently – and has short spiky hair which he dyes black. He has a cool squirrel-type of face. He's always jittery, talking to himself or to someone, but not us. He's the same age as me. His school finishes at about three p.m. Isn't that cool? I get home at seven p.m.

When we go skating Richie makes panda noises the whole way there and tells me that *Hore* is a word for a prostitute. Shit! Then, on the way back, he speaks in weird voices and just as we get to his house to drop him off, he looks at me and says, 'Nice night for walk,' like he's a Terminator.

Have you noticed how it's always Easter? I get a new watch. I always get a present near anything to do with Jesus because Mum is still trying to make me go to church and she thinks I'll give in if she buys me something. So, this year I go to church with them. Sausage's boyfriend, who is about two, like her, is in the choir and she keeps smiling at him. Well, she's about ten really. I got the watch a couple of days ago, before the swimming match. I was in a relay race with Richie, Reggie and another friend. Reggie was the best swimmer and me and him and Richie have an ace time. I like seeing these friends. They never say nasty stuff to me. Anyway, this new watch is waterproof and it's a digi. The numbers are on a screen and there are no hands. No hands at all. You can really see the numbers at night; there's this light on it and a stopwatch. You can watch the seconds tick away, although one number is hard to see because of the crack.

They took it off me and threw it around. They dunked it in water, thinking it would break and, for a moment, I was pleased they didn't know it was waterproof. They chucked it to each other and when it dropped on the floor it skidded back towards me. Just as I went to pick it up one of them stepped on it, cracking the glass.

I do not understand.

I picked it up. The one who stood on it asked me what I was going to do about it. I said, nothing. All I could think of was my Mum rustling in her purse for the twenty-pound note which this watch cost. The way she rustled it like Great Granny, when she was alive. And thinking about that nearly made me cry for some reason. But I didn't. Mum often reminds me of Great Granny. I remember, a few days before she died, she couldn't even pick up the Smartie tube: someone had to do it for her. She still ate them, though. They just took a bit longer for her to get down.

As I go to get my books for the next lesson I'm trying to remember who's in the class, and who I can avoid.

I know almost every subject, sport and hangout of everyone in my year, so I can be somewhere they're not. I don't mind sitting by myself for a few hours. I don't mind sitting by myself forever. I work out different routes around the school at different times of day to avoid bumping into them. Most of the time now I just sit by myself, looking out for them, checking my watch to see how long there is to go.

The stopwatch is still running: 5.40hrs, 34secs to go. I set my countdown every morning the minute I walk through the school gate. I look at it all day. I watch the last seconds tick away before it changes to 5.39 and clench my teeth, grind them. And the one who broke it knocks into me on purpose as he walks out of the room and I fall into the desk behind me and land on the floor. They laugh. All of them laugh. 5.37hrs, 57secs.

When my watch alarm beeps in the early evening I forgive everyone, like I do every day, and I leave the school. It was just a one-off. Tomorrow will be better. I only have five more years to go. But my watch only goes up to 12 hours at a time. I will reset it tomorrow when I wake up. Just for five more years.

5.

CAMOUFLAGE GHOSTS

The two most different things in the world are the Combined Cadet Force and roller skating with Marty. It isn't compulsory to join the CCF. But if you decide not to, which is completely your own choice, you're thought of as an outcast; it would be unlikely that you would manage A levels; you would have nothing to talk about at job interviews; you wouldn't get a place at university. And people would think you were a bender.

I didn't want to join. I don't mind the outdoor stuff. Me and Richie sometimes run down streams near my house and cook sausages which we puke up as they never do properly on our crap fire. That was okay, but I knew if I joined the CCF there would be two more times every week when I would be findable.

There are two men in charge: one is Australian, called Lieutenant Hedges and the other one is called something else. Lieutenant Hedges' nickname is Saccy. It's a few weeks until someone tells me it's because his face looks like a scrotum sac. It's a few more weeks until I find out that that means balls. All the corporals are boys in the sixth form. They often talk about the time when Colonel Wintle – that's the other one's name, I just remembered – got in a jeep with all of them and someone asked if he was a bit too drunk and he said, 'I might be too pissed to walk, but I'm not too pissed to drive.' They thought that was really funny. They could have put that on their Cadet Army badge as a kind of motto.

Lieutenant Hedges says he fought in a war and managed to defeat a lot of bloody Germans with his rusty penknife. He drinks a lot, his breath smells bad. He's unusual. Colonel Wintle is a huge man; he's big and tall with thick lips, greying hair that swishes back onto his head in a quiff. His lips, his fleshy nose, are made of the sort of ruddy, pored skin that only really rich people seem to have – their features popping out of their face. Whereas Lieutenant Hedges, Saccy, has the kind of skin that, well, you can imagine.

Wintle didn't drink as much as Saccy, but he was famous for that quote. That and walking into a chip shop after too many beers, getting his dick out onto the counter and saying, 'Batter that.' Everyone thought that was the funniest thing in the world. Everyone talks about their dicks the whole time, like they've just been given them. Colonel Wintle, he strides everywhere; he could probably walk across Britain in a few steps. He's roughly six times the size of me. The more stories he tells, though, the more people pay attention to him and not to me. It was lovely, the first week: everyone was so excited about having the opportunity to get booze and fags and start wars when they're older that they didn't notice me.

Twice a week I put on this scratchy uniform which is a shirt made from wild pig hair, I reckon, with a starched collar; Army issue trousers which are *so* uncomfortable, no one would wear them unless they had to; boots which have to be as reflective as mirrors, and something called puttees. A puttee is like a scarf for your ankle. You wind it round the top of your boot and tuck your trouser leg into it. It takes me about an hour to put two of these on and then they fall off within the first minute of running through a river.

We learn about teamwork; we learn how to get kicked in the balls by sixth formers; we learn to get our faces covered in shit (they'd shit in the tunnels you have to crawl through – just like in a real war!); we learn to shout and swear and stick our chests out like cocks in the morning.

'How's it smell down there?' Parry says, as we come out of a tunnel of shit.

'Why's there shit down there?' I ask.

'Because this is combat! What happens if there's another Falklands.'

'Why? Do Argentinians shit in tunnels?' I ask.

Then he kicks me in the balls, Parry does. He's the most evil person I have ever seen. He's fifteen or sixteen, I think. I won't forget him. *One day*, Parry. He's always somewhere behind me, shouting at me, telling me I'm a worthless piece of shit, in case I ever forget. It reminds me of that Vietnam film – except they were fighting in an Asian jungle and I'm running in circles, covered in shit, down by a disused cycle track in south-east England. And, whereas in Vietnam, I think they had to cook their own food and they were picked up in helicopters, we pop to the shop for a Twix afterwards and then are picked up by our parents.

Even my choice of chocolate bar makes them laugh

at me. There's something funny about Twix, about the car my mother drives, there's something funny about everything. In a way the CCF is better. They don't tease me – they're just hard and violent. And they call me things like, 'A little shit.' I don't mind that so much. Universal insults hurt so much less. It's when I'm called things that I don't know, or understand. It's those private jokes, the jokes they must have to work quite hard to come up with. They must spend a lot of time coming up with stuff about me. They must really not like me.

After two months of being in the Force I ask Colonel Wintle if I can leave. He tells me I signed up for two years, same as everyone else.

'Well, could I leave early?'

'In the army, son, you do your time. You do what your country expects of you, and you will be rewarded. Understand?'

'I'd rather go swimming in the afternoons. I have a chance to compete for the county. Can I leave please?'

'No.'

When Parry hears that I want to leave he starts giving me laps to run. I don't know if he's a prefect or not, but no one says no to him. So I have to come into school early in the mornings and run laps before assembly. He says it'll get me ready for the Night Exercise. When I first heard about this, a few weeks ago, I thought it fell on Cress's birthday and I couldn't eat any tea that night. We've been arguing a lot. She doesn't stop asking me what the matter is; it drives me nuts. She always wants to talk about things. So I thought I'd make it up to her and buy her a nice present or something. Anyway, the date was changed for the exercise, so I felt a bit better. This is an exercise when we go into the field. We go into *a* field. Then most of us have our first cigarette, throw up, then walk through a rainy night in the woods with ponchos on, making us look less like Clint Eastwood and more like tiny camouflage ghosts in a bad play. I'm just a ghost anyway, even without the poncho.

After six hours of solid walking our stops become more frequent so Parry can look at the map. We're lost. Every time we stop, a lot of us just collapse in the ditch. I don't even notice it's wet. After another hour I'm falling asleep for thirty seconds at each stop, falling onto the ground and sleeping for less than a minute, until someone picks me up by the scruff of the neck, and we start walking again.

Colonel Wintle is there to greet us at the end of our walk through the night. He stands up, tall like a tree, legs wide apart, his army arms crossed. He looks ten foot tall, like Odysseus in combat trousers. Parry has led us through the night, has kicked me in the shin. Someone told Parry that he wanted to bum Wintle and he went fucking mad. We stand around like a bunch of kittens who have been taken out of the river.

Wintle bellows, 'Hello men. Well done.'

I limp into the minibus.

'Right, off to Hoberton,' he shouts. Another couple of minibuses arrive. They drive us to Hoberton army base. Hoberton is barren, cold and looks like Russia probably did before the bloke with the birthmark took over. As we drive past the gates I can see some real army people

47

marching to orders. I listen in to the sergeant call out the marching. He's saying, '*Looft, height, looft, height, looft, height.*' He sounds like a Nazi. He looks up into our minibus and sees Wintle and salutes. It sends shivers down my spine. All the other boys are smiling, looking out of the coach window at the *real thing*, giving the thumbs up to everyone we pass. I look at the man saluting and I'm sure his eyes are cold enough to be a Nazi. We all get put into a big hangar where we're briefed.

Our first task, after no sleep, is to do the assault course. This is an assault course for Marines. I'm not a Marine, not even a man. I can't even jump high enough to get my hands onto the top of the first wall to haul myself up. This army guy who's taking us around the course helps me over it, but I can't reach the next obstacle. So I stand there, not knowing what to do with myself, with my hands. I feel awkward and stupid as I watch sweaty, hairy cadets jump up the walls, shouting at me as they pass. There's four feet between where my hands can reach and the top of the wall. I'm below everything. My neck is permanently cricked from looking up the whole time. The army guy in charge comes and helps me again. There's something so hard and indestructible about him – not like Wintle or Saccy – this man seems like he's made from harder material than me. He puts his hands under my shoulders and, standing behind me, throws me up towards the wall. I fly through the air, propelled by him. In flight I put my hands out, and as I start losing height I hook my hands onto the top of the wall, get a grip on it, and haul myself up. I look back once I'm standing on the wall and he nods at me. He's the only person I meet who shouldn't be shot instantly.

The next morning we're marched to breakfast. My boots are so small I can feel each of my toes blacken and rub against the sides. I mention to someone how the atmosphere is weird at this base. It wasn't the things we were doing: the assault course, the marching – that was all normal. It was the *looft, height* which made me feel weird. When we return to school, the school gates are vaguely more welcoming than the gates at the base. And I'm now a smoker – so something good has come out of it. I go home that evening and Mum asks me what it was like. I say it was tiring but rewarding. And character-building. That's what I was told it was. I'm not sure if my character is built just yet, though. Cress looks at me funny, as if I'd never say something like that. She's changed just since I last saw her. Her face seems to be changing; her hair is getting longer, changing style again; her eyes seem to be changing shape, or maybe it's her cheeks and face. Something is different about her – I don't know what the hell it is.

'Marlow, you never say very much any more,' Cress says, as I sit at the table and make a sandwich. Mum is cutting up carrots for later.

'You're very quiet,' Mum says. 'Everything all right?'

'Yeah.' I say.

Cress is off to a party so I sit and watch *Arthur* again. My new favourite bit is when Arthur's fiancée says, 'A real woman could stop you drinking.' He takes a swig of his whisky and says, 'It'd have to be a real big woman.'

49

I'm laughing by myself at that and I think about how there were no trees in Hoberton, as if anything that might have kept warmth in had to be removed. Cress comes back from her party with some cake.

'Watching *Arthur* again?'

'Yes.'

'Why're you so quiet?' she says, very directly while she absent-mindedly looks around the room for something.

'I don't know.'

'Is it school?'

I shrug and she stops asking questions. The army is everywhere I look. On the TV American aeroplanes drop bombs on Libya. There's a report we watch that says President Gaddafi's daughter was killed. I go and get the globe thing from the corner of the room and try and find Libya. I show it to Cress, who nods and carries on eating her cake. Mum says she has a strange metabolism. She eats but it's burnt away, or something. She's a funny-looking person, is Cress. She's got a huge gob and her lips look like she's been stung by a wasp. I wonder if I look weird as well.

After lunch is the time I hate the most. I'm sitting in the classroom by myself and my watch says it's 1.13 p.m. I click it over to see how many more hours I have to go before I can go home. I click it back. The classroom has desks all scored with aggressive swipes of compasses, scrawled ink insults. The room smells of wood or what-ever that classroom smell is. I sit there, as I do every day when everyone else is out walking around, sitting on the grass if the weather is nice, chatting to people.

I look out through the window and see three people from my class walking towards the classroom. I watch them as they walk along the horseshoe path that curves around the athletics pitch. They keep on coming and I'm waiting for them, any minute, to get distracted or to start off in another direction. This is a thousand times worse than an assault course. But they keep walking towards me, ready to break my peace and quiet. Finally, the outside door slams and I can hear them talking. I sit on the radiator behind the door and wait. The door flings open with force and smacks against the side of the radiator which makes me jump. I look down and notice that the door hit one of my fingers against the sharp edge of the radiator. My finger starts going black.

'What the fuck are you doing in here?'

'I'm just here.'

'So this is where you are every lunch-time,' one of them says.

'Why're you here?' another asks me.

'I'm just here.'

One of them asks me if I'm stealing stuff. I tell them I'm just waiting around for the lesson. He says, 'Budge up,' so he can sit on the radiator and then another one sits on it and then they all sit on it, crushing me up against the wall. Then they lean out on purpose. The first questions they ever asked me were just now. Normally they just make statements and accuse me of things. I wrench myself free from them and the radiator. As I stand up one of them lifts my fringe with one hand and slaps my forehead, shouting 'Slap head!' as he does it. They all laugh. Then another stands up and really quickly does the same. I laugh, feeling my head smart, and do the same back to one of them. The boy snarls at me and does it back to me, shouting 'Slap head!' really loudly again. I pretend to laugh; I don't know what else to do. Then I do it hard back to him and get him a bit in the eye which he makes a real fuss about. He gets me in a headlock and rams my head against one of the lockers, but it misses the top of my head and hits my eyebrow and soon I'm blinking quickly and I can feel blood drip out of my cut eyebrow like a leaking tap. I stand up, feel a bit dizzy and walk out into the bog. I get some toilet roll and wet it a bit and hold it up against my eyebrow. I normally call it a loo but they all call it a bog. I can hear them laughing in the classroom. I finish cleaning it all up and just stand there; if this eyebrow cut gets me ten minutes alone then it's been worth it. So I stand there and look at the wall. I can hear birds chirping away outside. That seems strange for some reason. This must be what prison is like: looking out and seeing sunshine and freedom but not being able to get there. When I look over at the door, one of them is standing there.

'Jesus, what the fuck is wrong with you?'

'I hit my eyebrow.'

'I know that, I was there. No, you were just standing there, in a trance, and your head was wonky and you were breathing funny.'

'No I wasn't.'

'Yes, you were. Weirdo. Anyway, this was all a joke, yeah? You aren't gonna be a gay and tell anyone.'

I shake my head.

52

I stay there a little bit longer. I have to fill the bowl with water and dunk my whole head in it as the bog roll has dried in the blood on my eyebrow and it won't come off.

Before I go home, a teacher asks me what's wrong with my eye. I tell him that I tripped and fell. He mumbles and asks me what class I'm in. An hour later I go to get into the car. When I climb in, Mum is looking worried. She looks me up and down and her face looks scared.

'What's the matter?' I ask her. I work out what I'll tell her if she asks about my eyebrow. I'll tell her I fell over.

'Um, Marlow,' she says. 'I'm afraid . . . Lizzer died this morning.'

'She died,' I say, like a statement.

'I found her in the tank, she was lying very still. I think she had a stroke, if lizards can have strokes.'

'Oh,' I say.

'Are you okay?' she asks.

'Yes,' I say.

'MARLOW!' A scream makes me jump.

'What?'

'Marlow, I've been saying your name a thousand times. What's the matter?' Mum asks. I look out through the car window. We are home.

'Nothing.'

'So nothing's the matter,' she says, shaking her head, fiddling the keys out of the ignition. When I get in I sit by myself and read the paper with the television on.

'You don't read the paper,' Cress says, skipping into the room.

'Shut up.'

'Buggershit,' she says, then puts her hand over her mouth, her eyes widening, amazed and impressed by what she just said.

'Do you want something?' I ask.

'I feel weird today.'

'I feel weird every day.'

There's a story on the fourth page about how four corporals are going to be disciplined for making young recruits march naked in the snow at six in the morning. It was one of many reports of bad treatment of cadets at the Hoberton army base. I take my shoes off and look at the blackened ends of my toes from those boots.

6.

COUGH

As the first year comes to an end, I go up to Danny and hope that I can see him on the holidays. Maybe we can be friends again. He says, 'Go away, queer,' and then he phones me the first day of the holidays to see if I want to go canoeing with him. As this is the last day of term we have to go for our medical. All people who have joined the school that year have to do it. I walk in for mine before lunch. The matron is fat, with a watch outside her pocket, and her fingernails are bitten right down. She looks like she tried to dye her hair but it came out really badly. I have memorised the list of my year, in the order it was put up on the noticeboard, for the medical. That way, as I know what subjects they'll be doing just before and after, I can plan my route so I don't see any of them.

I walk into the examination room, take my trousers off and my blazer and my shirt and I stand there.

She says, 'Right, the first thing to do is to weigh you and measure you.'

I stand up against the wall and she makes a mark above my head on the tape, stuck to the wall. Then she asks me to stand on the scales. She takes a note of how much I weigh.

'Your dad.'

'Yes.'

'How tall is he?'

'Over six foot.'

'Do you look like him?' she asks, like she's covering up the fact that she asked about how tall he was for a reason.

'I'm not sure. I don't see him much. He's away on business.'

'What's he doing?' she says taking out one of those inner-tube things which goes around your arm.

'He's in Holland.'

'Very nice,' she says. 'And your mum?'

'She's a dwarf.'

She doesn't hear that and carries on taking my blood pressure. She asks me what sports I play and I tell her I like squash and I like basketball.

'I won't be a minute,' she says. 'I just want the doctor to have a look at you.'

The doctor comes in and says hello. He asks me how old I am. He says my voice hasn't broken yet. In case I hadn't noticed. He asks me to take my pants down which I do and then he asks me to do all the coughing stuff which I do.

'You know, boys come to puberty at all different ages,' he says. I'm just about to go, when the bloody matron thing comes back in like she's just thought of something important. She asks me to stand up straight and looks me up and down. Then she asks me to walk in a straight line, which I don't do very well. She looks at the way I walk. One foot is sticking out at a strange angle, she says. She asks me if I'd noticed it before. I tell her I haven't. She makes me sit down and takes my foot in her hand. It hurts when she presses it.

'You know, you have a lot of very tiny bones in your foot. I think you might have one which is broken in here.'

So the doctor comes *back* in and has a look and says he thinks it's broken too. I remember a game of stamps that we were having the week before. What you have to do is stamp on someone's foot. I didn't win. She looks me up and down and she seems a bit worried for some reason.

Matron says, 'You've been in the wars a bit haven't you?'

'Not really.'

'Your eye, your foot.'

'Not really.'

'Sometimes it's what's said, though, isn't it? It's what's said rather than the physical stuff, which really hurts, isn't it?' she says, looking right at me. 'So, d'you have a girlfriend?'

'Are you joking?' I say.

'You. Do. *Like*. Girls . . . though,' she says.

'Not really,' I say, trying not to laugh.

'Oh, I mean, I'm sure they're annoying. But you think they're pretty, don't you?'

'No,' I say. She looks worried and looks at her watch that's on her white coat, resting on her gynormous tits. 'Have you ever had any dreams about, about your friends?' she says.

'Which friends?' Then I get bored of the game. 'Don't worry I'm not a bender,' I say. That shuts her up for a moment. I think about what it was like taking Lizzer out of her tank, all cold and stiff with a tiny bit of blood on her head. The other lizard – the one Granny bought me – stayed right at the other end of the tank. I took Lizzer out and put her in a big CD carton, one of the ones which American CDs come in – a present from my pen pal Garry, in California. Everyone asked if they could help me but I said I wanted to do it by myself. When I got out into the garden there was already a hole dug. I put the box in there, my little dead lizard inside a *Megadeth* CD box. It was their first album: *Killing is my business and business is good*. There's wicked guitaring on that album. I filled the hole in with the mud and then sat down. After a couple of minutes I looked beside me and Cress was sitting there.

'Is she in there?' she asked.

'Yes.'

'Even though she was disgusting and I hated her, I *will* miss her,' Cress said, sweetly.

'I know. Me too.'

Then Cress patted the soil mound covering the hole, and a tear came to her eye.

'Can I go?' I ask. Matron nods and gives me a note to give to someone but I throw it away. I walk out of the medical office and set my watch. I take out a tissue and wipe where the goo is coming out of the cracked face of my watch. The sellotape I've put over it hasn't worked. I have five weeks and ten hours holiday, which starts in two hours. I can't even manage two more hours. I feel so tired, like I can't keep my eyes open, but I have to, I have to keep watch. So I walk out of the school grounds and head towards the bus stop. I have a look at the timetable, and realise there's nowhere particular for me to go. I think about Peri and how I can see her. I look at my watch: one and three quarter hours to go. I get on the bus and sit on it for twenty minutes. I know where I am. I get out of the bus, and walk over to the public playing fields, my fingers crossed in my pockets. As I get nearer I can see girls playing hockey at one end. I keep walking. I stick on my home coat, so they can't see what school I'm from. As I get almost to the pitch I see her. I see Peri. She's trying to beat some girl with her hockey stick, shouting, 'You bitch,' really loudly. The teacher separates them. Peri is so cool. This is a great start to the holidays. The teacher is shouting at her and pointing, telling her to get off the pitch. She does, but she walks away from where I am. She can't see me. I watch her walk back to her school, probably to detention. The teacher notices me, so I quickly get out of there, and hop on the next bus back to school. When I get back I still have ten minutes left to go, so I sit down on a bench with my fists clenched in tension, and wait for everything to finish.

7.

THE GARAGE

I'm sick tonight. It's the last day of holidays before term starts again. It's probably the prawns which disagreed with me. We had a special meal last night, like we normally do and watched *Arthur*. Peri and her sister Lucy came round. Lucy and Cress went upstairs and talked about all kinds of things that are probably illegal. Peri watched *Arthur* with me and told me it was crap the whole time. It was nice to see her: I only get to see her from time to time because she's a boarder at her school and she keeps beating people up. She hates it. We both hate it. While we talk, Mum keeps coming in and asking Peri where Cress is, like she'd know. Peri's mum is late to pick them up, and she doesn't look well; her eyes look all red. In the end the three of them take a taxi home, and leave their car at our house. I go to bed, but hardly sleep. When I wake up early this morning, I'm sick again but I don't tell anyone about that. I wish I was old. If I was eighty then people would leave me alone and forget about me and I could just sit somewhere and read magazines.

On the way to school, Mum keeps asking me what Peri and I talked about. As I get out of the car Mum doesn't give me a hug; she's daydreaming I think. The first day back after the holidays is careers day. It's great, everything seems fine. No one says anything to me, nothing nasty all morning. When it all starts up again at lunch-time I remember that I hadn't seen anyone in the morning apart from careers people.

After lunch I go to see Grim. He sits there like something that's died but the cobwebs have kept alive. Grim is only his nickname, and he's sitting there like an old bastard with these little spectacles on his nose, in an old suit which I bet even the moths have left alone. Sometimes, last term, I'd watch him drive his car out of the gates. His face was scrunched up against the windscreen he was leaning so far forward, his foot on the accelerator and clutch at the same time. That car used to rev like hell, and by the time he got to the end of the school drive the windscreen wipers were going on full throttle. He never managed to find the indicator. I heard he used to retire every year, and then come back three months later. He was into his third comeback. He must have liked the decanters he always got as leaving presents.

Grim says, 'Yes now, so you did the career test last term, we've got the results.' He pulls out a piece of paper and hands it to me. He looks at his copy. It says I'm ideally suited to being a policeman or working in a hotel.

'What do you think?' he asks.

'I don't know,' I tell him. I say that I don't like policemen very much and I don't like hotel food.

'Well, what *do* you like doing?'

'Nothing.'

'Well, what about catering?'

'What, food?'

62

'No, catering. What degree do you think you would like to do?'

'I don't know if I *will* do one.' I'd only do it if I could go to a college in Scotland or Iceland. Where none of them would be. 'It won't be for five years anyway,' I say. Hopefully I'll be dead by then.

'But it's important to start thinking about it.' He takes out a load of pamphlets, 'If you do go to university you're then in an *elite* group of people and you can have whichever job you choose.'

'Things might change after, um, eight years from now when I could finish university.'

'They won't. I can promise you that university is like a badge of honour,' he says, getting louder, 'which you can wear and wear proudly. Like the badge for this school.'

'Right.'

'And don't forget 1992.'

'What?'

'When you choose your A levels. You know, French and Business Studies is a great combination. Lots of things will change in 1992 and if you can't speak French you'll never get a job. We'll be overrun by those buggers,' he says out of the corner of his mouth, like it's a secret for just him and me.

'Right.'

'Are you a monitor or a prefect?'

'I'm fourteen.'

'Of course. But you could become a monitor next year and then a prefect later on. Universities love to see that you're involved with people and leadership.'

'I don't want to be a prefect; they don't seem to be nice people.'

He doesn't hear that.

'I keep lizards?' I say.

He ignores that.

'Are you in the CCF?'

'Yes, but I don't like it.'

'Good chap. Businesses love an army man.'

I suddenly remember what I was going to say to him. 'I enjoy drawing.'

'Well, there you go. You could be a, er . . . are you sure you don't want to be a policeman?'

'I think that would be too stressful for me. I like drawing, music.'

'Well,' says Grim, bored now, 'whatever you choose, having been in the CCF and being a monitor—'

'I'm not a monitor.'

'But you *will* be. Those two things will stand you in good stead for any profession. Constable was in the CCF, I believe.'

'A policeman?'

'No, the painter. Constable. Landscapes. Look, if a university gets two applications from two fine people who've both done French and Business then who do you think they'd take?'

'I don't know.'

'The one who was in the CCF, of course. The one who was a prefect.'

The one who has crawled through tunnels of shit.

'Right,' I say for about the millionth time.

'Okay, what sports do you like?' he says, trying to

start a conversation. 'Cricket? Football?'

'I like skating.'

'Ice skating?'

'No, roller skating.'

'So you don't like any team sports?'

'I like basketball.'

He looks me up and down. 'How tall are you?'

'Five foot?'

'If *that*, I should say. You're a bit small for basketball, aren't you?'

I go to leave. As I do, he pipes up.

'You do seem to have an anti-authority streak in you. That's not good. You need to fall into line to succeed in this world.'

'What about Hemingway?'

'What year is he in?'

'The writer.'

'Well, Hemingway was very big. You aren't. But you can build character through the cadet force and through supporting your school, and when you get in the real world you have to do a lot of things you don't like.'

I stop listening. I don't hate him, though. He's not a nasty man, just a total dick splash. He's one of the better ones. At my last school *only* two of the teachers got the sack for trying to touch up boys. Pretty good eh? Whereas here no one has got done since I've been here. But there's something else going on, something a bit weird which I've only really understood after a year here. It's the way some teachers look up to the popular boys – usually the sports captains – as heroes. It seems weird that they want a friendship between the boy and

65

themselves. And I just wonder if it's because they don't talk to other adults very much. At my last school, there were teachers who *loved* to scare us. And I think back now, three years ago, to a teacher who made a kid stand on his desk, facing the class for the whole lesson, until he finally started crying.

I bunk off the next hour of careers day and walk up into the town. I was told I wasn't allowed to, but punishment is better than being there. In the café I bump into Danny's brother – the one who bought Iron Maiden before anyone else. He's selling pot to people in the café and he buys me a cup of tea. He listens to what I say. He must be at least eighteen.

'Marlow, don't worry about this shit. D'you know what a microcosm is?'

'Spunking?'

Danny's brother spits his Coke back into the glass, tries to stop laughing.

'Okay, you know when sometimes you can have a world within a world?'

'Not really.'

'Don't try and pretend to be thick, Marlow. You probably do that at school, don't you? I know damn well you know what I'm talking about. Don't be like Danny – what a little shit he's become. Little bastard ... anyway ... um ... shit,' he forgets what he was saying, '... got to stop smoking ...'

'So what d'you think is the problem with those teach-ers – the ones who got the sack, the ones who humiliated boys in front of the class?'

'Well, definitely for those male teachers I think it's the

real world outside the school which scares the shit out of them. They can't handle that, so they create a little world where they're king. But who wants to be King of the Munchkins . . . what?'

'Nothing.'

'You were going to say Dorothy wanted to be Queen of the Munchkins, weren't you?'

'No.'

'Yes.'

'Yes, I was.'

'You've got that humour, Marlow. You should . . . um . . . shit, what were we talking about?'

'The Queen of the Munchkins.'

'The munchies?'

'Munch*kins.*'

'Oh, yeah. You should use your humour from time to time – might help.'

A teacher walks past the front of the café. Danny's brother stands up, so the teacher can't see me. He sits back down.

'We were talking about teachers,' I say.

'I remember when I was in the sixth form. If I think about half of those male teachers, they were real bastards to the girls who were seventeen or eighteen. And you know why?'

'Why?'

'Because those girls were just about old enough to scare them. So they got over it by being bastards to them; and with the younger boys they played power games, I mean power games with a room full of people forty years younger than themselves . . .'

'How do you know all this?'
'That's classified. You want some pot?'
'Which one is pot?'

I wander back to school, feeling better. After we've had our personal session with Grim we have to go and listen to some people from the army do a talk in the afternoon. They say that although there's no war going on at the moment there actually is. And it's the Russians who are the enemy. And when we're all old then probably the Chinese will be the enemy. And we need to value our freedom. They hand out leaflets about who are the most dangerous foreigners.

'I didn't know they had lots of gold in the Soviet Union,' someone says.

'Cold. It's the *Cold* War,' a woman army officer says, handing him a poster of a man running through the jungle with a gun. Doesn't look like Russia to me.

'What d'you think about the guy with the mark on his head?' I ask someone as we walk out of the building.

'He seems all right,' they say.

'D'you think there's going to be a war?' I ask. 'With Ronald Reagan.'

'Don't reckon.'

'Do you think America wants a war,' I ask. He looks bored.

'Why would a country ever *want* a war?' he says, and runs off to start the afternoon scrap with the kids from the other school in the town. After lunch, I go and read a book. Aldridge, my housemaster, comes up to me.

'Can I have a word?' he asks.

I follow him into his office. He says that the matron had told him about my medical at the end of last year but he didn't have enough time to talk to me before the holidays. He asks me what happened with my foot and I tell him it was just a game, and with my eye it was playing football which I'm not any good at. I got my foot sorted out in the holidays.

I tell him things are not the same as they were. He asks me to expand on that and I shrug. He says that all things change. I say I used to like my last school and this one I don't like at all, no offence or anything, but I really hate it and I don't like the people. He says that it's still early, I should give it some time to settle in, to join in with my peers. He says I shouldn't try to become a carbon copy of them, but I should try to find a way of fitting in. I say that I used to fit in fine with them, we used to mess about together and now I'm a stranger. His face looks like a damp potato. He's sweaty.

'You have a scholarship to the school, you're *very* lucky. I should make the most of it,' he says. 'You should talk to me about these problems.' Then he says something about loco parentis. He's a dick splash as well. I walk out of the room.

I'm not really noticeable, barely even visible, anymore.

The next day I go to my lessons as usual. The chanting carries on. It picks up. I can hear it wherever I go – they just quietly chant something and then laugh when I walk in the room. No teachers notice it. There are other things that they say as well. Some of them seem to be in code, I don't know what they mean. When I try to answer them, they laugh again. There are things which I don't want to tell you.

Then there are times during which I can almost forget completely about school and all those people. It reminds me of when I was little. Just having fun. Quite often me, Marty and Richie get videos out in the evenings, when I get back from school. I look along the rack and pick up *First Blood*, look at Richie. He pretends to sew his arm on and groans. Then he shakes his head. He looks excited. He takes *Porky's* down from the rack.

'Are we gonna get away with this?'

Richie goes up the aisles of the video library, doing strange walks. He picks up a video box, there's a man on the front, his huge arms and hands holding the bars of a prison. Richie points to me, 'You're goin' down to do two by four! In solitary!'

'It's two *to* four,' Marty says. Marty has *Lemon Popsicle* in his hand. 'Tell Marlow what happened with Helen last night.'

'What?' Richie looks all innocent.

'Tell him. Or are you all embarrassed?'

'I comes home, shags the missus, wipes me dick in the curtains, she *'its* the roof,' Richie says.

'He snogged this girl he likes last night,' Marty says.

'What's she like?' I ask. He looks embarrassed and doesn't say anything.

'He's all shy now,' Marty says.

'I'll kill you with my vice-like grip,' Richie says and jumps on Marty. They roll around on the floor until the owner of the video shop tells them to get up and get out. We rent *Porky's* before we leave. We sit and watch it; Marty and Richie shout and do voices while it's on. Laughing feels strange; it feels wrong. I sit there pretty quietly. Marty goes home after the film.

'So what about this girl then?' I ask Richie.

'Helen,' Richie says.

'What's she like?'

'Nice. She's nice,' he looks a bit emotional. He puts on a smile and runs out of things to say.

'Do you love her?' I joke.

'Don't know. She's really . . . I don't know. Maybe?'

I probably look shocked. This is Richie's first girl-friend and he's only kissed her once, and she told him to take his hands out of his pockets while they were doing it. So he put them behind his back as he didn't know what to do.

'Helen's got a friend, she likes you,' he says.

'How come? She hasn't met me.'

'I *told* her about you, idiot,' Richie looks at me like I *am* an idiot. I think I would like to live in Richie's world.

'What's she like?'

Richie shuffles from one foot to the other, then grins from ear to ear, he screws his face up and says, 'Flaps like John Wayne saddlebags.'

'What does that mean?'

'I dunno,' he says.

'There's sort of someone I like,' I say. I freeze – feel like I've given something away, made myself open. I wait for the attack. Richie just smiles.

'That's cool,' he winks.

I wake up in the morning and think about Richie's sayings. I smile and then bend over with pains in my stomach. By the time I get to the school gate, the night before with Marty and Richie has completely gone from my memory. After lunch, I go to walk over to the classroom but I can see them over there; I can see people moving about in the classroom. Normally they would never be over there. So I turn around. I think the same thing I think about every day. But today I do it.

I walk out of the school gates. I leave the school and walk along the road, past the shops, which look different, more interesting and exotic at 2 p.m., when I would never normally see them. I walk past the café. I watch people moving around, going about whatever they're going about. I realise I look like I've just walked out of school, so I take my blazer off and throw it in a rubbish bin. Then I take my tie off and do the same. Then I go back, pick my blazer out of the bin, crumple it up into a ball, and carry it under my arm. I walk for two miles, which takes ages, and for half a mile or so there's no path really and no shops. But then the shops start again and I can see the garage in the distance, so I make for it. I look at my watch. It's 3.15 p.m. I've been out of school for over an hour and I can feel something in my chest, something which feels nice, like I can breathe better. My eyesight seems better, too. I take two deep breaths, remember what it feels like to not cramp up when I try and breathe in. Little breaths make me less noticeable.

72

I keep on walking until I reach the garage. I go straight into the workshop when I get there. There's no one around. I can hear someone drilling in the workshop next door but I can't see anyone. A radio is on in the background. It's playing that song: *I don't want to set the world on fire.* On the wall, there's a poster which says 'Welcome to Paradise.'

Then I see him, standing, looking a bit vacant, in front of me.

'What're you doing here?' Dad says.

'I came to see you.'

'Shouldn't you be at school?'

A thin, tall man walks round. He's called Peter.

'Oh, hello Marlow. What're you doing here? Come to see your dad?'

'Yeah,' I say. Dad looks half-asleep. He puts his arm around me and winks at Peter and takes me into the reception area. He lights a cigarette. He hasn't shaved today and he's wearing a boiler suit.

'Are you skipping school?'

'I've left.'

'For good?' he almost looks proud. He smiles. 'What's going on, half day?'

'No, I've walked out.'

'Bloody hell,' he says.

He has oil on his face from where he keeps wiping the sweat away with his hands. 'Why're you looking at me so closely?' he asks.

'I'd forgotten what you looked like,' I say. He looks really shocked by that. I didn't mean anything by it. He looks really taken aback. 'Will you phone the school

73

and tell them I'm leaving?' I ask. There are pictures on the walls of blonde women with big tits, lying topless on beaches. The place smells of oil, and the floor has slippery patches on it. The radio keeps going in and out of tune.

'You know I don't have time to think about this sort of stuff, Marlow, I'm really busy.'

'Please Dad,' I say. I think I'm crying now. He comes over and puts his arms around me. 'I never see you,' I say.

'You will see me more now I'm doing this job,' he says, kindly. I stop crying. Feel better. 'Look, I've just got to finish one thing quickly, I won't be a minute.'

'Why aren't people allowed in the workshop?' I ask him. He shrugs.

'It's hard to describe,' he says. He goes into the workshop and I follow him. His head goes back under the bonnet of this car. 'This job, it's a bit like . . .' His voice is tight as he struggles with something in the engine '. . . it's like . . . being a doctor . . . except, these are cars and doctors work with . . .' he pulls hard at something in the engine '. . . bodies.' Suddenly, a piece of metal comes off in his hand and water or something spurts vertically into the air and showers down, soaking us. He stands there, under the spray. He stands there, dead still. Then he talks, calmly.

'Well, that's fucked it,' he says and bursts out laughing. I can't remember him ever laughing. He really laughs, his face goes red. I laugh too. I don't know why I do, though.

'Is this why people aren't allowed in here?' I ask. That

makes him laugh even more. He manages to stop the water coming out, then takes me back into the reception. He calls Mum.

'Hi, it's me. Yeah, he's with me. *You* phone them. Okay I will,' he says and then hangs up the phone.

'I have to phone the school.' He gets out the phone book, for a minute he can't remember the name he's looking for, then he dials the number. He asks to speak to Aldridge.

'Hullo, I'm calling about Marlow Walker. Yeah, it's his father here. Yes, he's with me. Okay, bye.'

We get in the car and he drives me back to school and Aldridge asks him to have a chat but he says he has to get back to work. He says he'll pop in when he comes to pick me up, which he never does. I go to the final half hour of my last lesson. One of them whispers over to me, 'Where've you been?'

'Nowhere,' I say.

I come out of the lesson and phone the garage. 'Can you come and pick me up?'

'I only dropped you off half an hour ago.'

'I know. I only had half an hour left. And my clothes are still wet.'

That night the four of us sit at the table: Dad, me, Cress and Mum. We're waiting for the *Oh la la*s to arrive for dinner.

'You know, when I phoned Mr Aldridge today, Marlow, to say Dad would be driving you back to school, he said he thought your father was away on business. In Holland. Why would he say that?'

'Because he's mad.' I say. The *oh la la*s arrive. They're called Donald and Heather Mottishead. We sit and eat our lasagne.

'We miss you at the paper, Doyle,' Donald says.

'I don't miss any of you at all,' he says. He looks serious.

Donald laughs, 'We miss your kidding, see? Like that. We're looking forward to having you back.'

'Stress is strange, isn't it?' Heather whispers. 'Many of my patients . . .'

Mum *shushes* Heather who stops.

'He's just tired,' Mum says.

'Why aren't you lying on a beach then, Doyle?' Donald says. 'John on the news desk has just been to Antigua on a really good deal. I would've thought you'd want to get away for your sabbatical.'

'Because I hate beaches and I like cars and it relaxes me to fix things with my hands. I can do it. I can see the result. I can hear and drive the result. I just like it.'

'Each to their own,' Donald says, with a smirk.

'John on the news desk has an ulcer,' Heather says.

'Really?' Mum says.

'Exactly!' Dad says.

'How long will you be away from the paper do you think? Or are you taking one day at a time?' Heather says.

'I'm not sure,' Dad says.

'Do you . . . *know* someone at the garage?' Donald seems really confused.

Dad looks pissed off. 'Yes.'

76

'Friends?' he jokes, as if Dad wouldn't be friends with mechanics.

'Old friends,' Dad says seriously and looks right at Donald.

Donald looks edgy and tries to change the subject, 'I'll tell you one thing. I took my car in the other day just to have a new clutch cable put in and when I came to pick it up they'd done two things I hadn't asked for *and* charged me for it. "Well," I said, "I'm not paying for that!"'

'What happened?' Mum asks. Dad raises his eyes to heaven.

'They told me that I had to pay because the work had already been done. So I looked at this chap and I said: "Listen here, I don't give a ..."' he looks around the room like he always does when he's going to swear, '"... a shit,"' he whispers, then stops for a second, 'Sorry Marlow,' he puts his hand on mine then continues his story, 'I said, "I will *not* pay for it."' He sort of says sorry again, as if I would die because he said shit. He doesn't even notice Cress over there. Mind you, her head barely comes up to the top of the table because she's leaning over, trying to feed bits of tomato to the stray cat she's not supposed to let inside.

There's a pause in the conversation.

'Well, that told them,' Dad says, with a funny expression in his voice, like he doesn't mean it.

'I must say, you don't look ill,' Heather says to Dad.

'I don't feel *ill*,' Dad says.

The Mottisheads go early as they have a new dog which eats the curtains. They had to change their last one because it clashed with the new carpet. As we clear up, Peri and her sister come round. Peri sits in the kitchen with me. Mum calls me from the sitting room. I walk in, she's watching the television.

'I should go upstairs, love. Finish your homework. I think Peri would like to spend some time with a girl; you know what they're like.'

'Oh, okay.'

I go upstairs and sit in my room. After five minutes Peri walks into my room.

'What are you doing in here?' I say, quietly.

'Where did you go? I don't want to talk to your sister. Is that the Silver Surfer?' She points to a poster on my wall. I start showing her some comics but I can hear my mother call me and Cress from downstairs. Peri and I walk back into the kitchen.

'I hear that you can do confirmation classes at school,' Mum says.

'Oh.'

'So if you find out when they start—'

'I'm not sure if I want to do confirmation classes,' I say. Another few hours when I'll be available to them, open, noticeable. What would they say?

'It's not whether you *want* to do it, you are *going* to do it.'

'I don't believe in God, either,' Peri says. I smile at her.

'Of course you do,' Mum says, 'You've a lovely family.'

Dad walks into the room.

'Doyle, tell him about confirmation classes.'

'What about them?'

'You did them, I was just saying that it's something which we'd like him to do.'

'I don't know,' Dad says.

'Sorry?' Mum sounds annoyed. 'Marlow, we'll talk about this tomorrow.'

Then she changes, 'It might be something you could get involved in,' she says.

'I don't think that's the kind of thing . . .' Dad starts and his voice trails off. Mum sits by me, 'Why did you run away today. What were you thinking?' She's forgotten Peri is there.

'I just, you know. I don't like school.'

'What don't you like about it?'

'I don't know.'

'It'll get better, I promise,' she says.

'School is rubbish and so is God,' Peri announces.

'A right couple of anarchists we've got here,' Dad says. 'You're made for each other.' Mum looks daggers at him, as Granny Two would say. Cress comes in with Lucy. They look like two demons.

'And what have you two been up to?' Dad asks. They both smile and say nothing.

'What do you think of school?' Dad asks them.

'This is just asking for trouble,' Mum says.

'Freedom of speech,' Dad says. 'What do you two crazed elves think of it, then?' he asks the girls.

'I like it,' Cress says. Lucy nods and smiles in agreement, looks shy and sucks her finger.

On Sunday it was written that we all have to go to

church. I sit in the kitchen with Mum, while Cress and Dad get ready. Dad was ill this morning and nearly couldn't go, but suddenly he got better.

'What's the difference between us and Catholics?' I ask.

'Not now, Marlow.'

'How come Roman Catholics have the Pope and the Vatican, and we have Brian with bad breath and the village hall?'

'Because all we need is the village hall. Jesus only had a village hall.'

'Did he have bad breath?'

'Marlow!'

'When in the Bible was he in a village hall?' I ask.

'With the tax men, when he threw them out,' she says.

'That wasn't a village hall,' Dad says, walking into the room.

'Is that what you're wearing?' Mum asks him.

'No, I'm wearing this for the car, but I'll put my wet suit on before we go into the church,' he says.

'Who's the Muslim man?' I ask.

'Muhammad,' Dad says.

'Who's the one on the news all the time?'

'Oh, do you mean the Ayatollah?' Dad says. 'Have you been doing that at school?'

'No. I saw it on the telly.'

'Don't they teach you stuff at school about other countries? Do you do world religions and things like that?'

'Don't they believe the same as us?'

'There you go,' Dad says, looking at Mum. 'You pay all that money and all he's taught is about one tiny island off the coast of France with a village hall religion.'

'We don't pay *any* money, and we really must go,' she says.

Dad shuffles off and comes back with a book. He hands it to me. 'Read this, Marlow, and tell your teachers to wake up.'

'He's a bit young for politics, Doyle.'

'Doesn't hurt to read, does it? What are you doing now? Have you done about the Falklands?'

'No. We're doing Bannockburn.'

'Bloody hell,' Dad says.

'Look,' Mum says to me, 'I was brought up Church of England, and you'll be Church of England. No one is going to convert today; we're just going to church like a normal family.'

'But not many people are Church of England. So there must be something wrong with it,' I say.

'You know, Marlow,' Dad says, looking poetic, 'there are many religions and a lot of wars have been fought in the name of them, and some damn fine buildings have been built in the name of them.'

'Are the speeches over?' Mum says.

'Does the Pope eat pizza?' Cress asks, standing in the doorway. She looks glamorous.

'Look at my beautiful daughter,' Dad says.

'I've no idea,' Mum says to Cress. 'How is this relevant? Why do we have to have all these questions every Sunday? Everyone in the car.'

The four of us sit in the service. I look at how high Mum and Dad come up to, on the backs of the long church benches. My shoulders are only just level with Dad's arms. Cress is getting taller, too. I can't see in front of me as someone's head is in the way. I sit and listen to the vicar who says that our prayers should be with the troubled countries of the world which are at war. He mentions some names, and Dad leans over. 'Ask your teachers about these places,' he whispers. Mum nudges him to be quiet. We sing some drony hymns. I can't hardly stand to sing them, they sound so damp and dead. Everyone here is old. Cress keeps winking at one of the choirboys, who can't stop smiling. The vicar does a reading from the Bible, I think it was St Paul. Cress leans in towards me, and puts her mouth by my ear. I get a strange feeling; she's wearing perfume I think. She whispers, 'I'm bored,' but there's something weird about her voice; there's something strange about her. It's like she's been given some kind of weird power. I don't know. She moves away and looks at me, her eyes all big.

'Tell Dad I don't feel well and you're taking me outside for some air.'

'Are you insane—'

Mum *shushes* me.

'Are you insane?' I whisper.

'Please,' she says, looking right at me. I don't know what happens but I find myself telling Dad that I'm taking Cress outside. He looks surprised and then says, 'Don't be long.'

We shuffle to the end of the row. I make sure I don't

catch Mum's eye as we walk down the aisle to the door. We get outside.

'You really feel ill?' I ask.

'No.'

'Well, there's nothing to do out here. What are we doing here?'

Cress shrugs.

'Why did you make me do this?' I say, laughing. Cress shrugs again. We wait a few minutes and go back in. Cress does a great impression of someone who's been ill. Mum buys it. The vicar is just finishing St Paul, and we have one more hymn, the one about 'strength and shield' where there's always some joker who does the echo. Then we're out of there. As we walk out of the service Mum turns to me, 'You'll be able to come up and take communion with us, when you're confirmed.'

'I'm not sure if I want to,' I say.

'If I'd had the choice I wouldn't have got confirmed,' Dad says. 'Maybe we should leave it up to him. If he feels he has the belief one day then he'll do it for the right reasons.'

'Don't use language like that in a church. Christ! Doyle, what is the matter with you? *Do it for the right reasons* . . . that's no way to go about it. He'll never do it that way.'

Dad says, 'Then maybe he shouldn't if he doesn't want to. He's never liked church, you couldn't even get him to those Christingle services and they're a lot more fun than this crap.'

'Don't say "crap". This is a church.'

'Did Doyle say "crap"?' Cress asks.

'His name is *Dad*. No darling. He said "crab",' Mum
says. 'He cannot just shirk his responsibilities and drop
out. We can't *all* always do the things we like the
whole time,' she says, looking at Dad, scowling. He
glares back. She turns. 'Lovely service,' she says to the
vicar as we walk past him and shake his hand. He has
a weak handshake. He smiles at Dad.

'And how are you feeling?' he asks, earnestly.

'Better now it's over,' Dad says. The vicar doesn't
know what he's referring to. He shakes Cress's hand
vigorously and says he likes her outfit. On the way
home Cress asks if we can take a detour to some shop
so she can buy a blank tape to record the Top 40 on
the radio.

'We've got plenty at home,' Mum says. Dad carries on
driving. Cress leans forward from the back seat, puts her
arms around Dad from behind.

'Daaad,' she says.

'What?'

'Can we stop so I can get a blank tape?'

'Er, which shop?'

'There are enough at home,' Mum says. 'Let's get
back.'

'Please Dad,' she says, ruffling her nose in his hair.

The detour takes an extra half hour. As Cress bounces
out of the car to get the tape I can see Dad smile
to himself. He thinks no one can see him, and says
something like, 'bloody women' affectionately, under
his breath, as he watches her get three Dixon's assistants
running around finding tapes.

*   *   *

'We hear your father isn't away on business,' Aldridge says at school on Monday.

'Oh,' I say.

'He recently left his job, because of . . . *tiredness*,' he says. 'There's nothing wrong with that. We all get tired. I have a friend who you might like to talk to. He's very clever and very nice.'

'Okay,' I say.

'Sometimes, people who are unhappy create another, alternative world to protect themselves. Do you know what I mean?'

'Do you think those Ethiopians do that?'

'What have they got to do with it?'

'I should think they're more unhappy than me.'

His friend turns out to be a psychiatrist or astrologer or whatever they call them. He has a bald head and talks quite slowly and quietly.

'Have you always felt left out?' he asks.

'No, I never used to.'

'And what about your sister?'

'What about her?'

'Do you talk to her, has she said anything to you that would upset you?'

'I don't know what you mean.'

He looks a bit strange. 'And your father is not well?'

'He's fine. We're all fine. Why d'you want to know about my sister? What have they all got to do with this? Are you gonna tell them about what I've been saying?'

'Calm down, now, who do you mean *them*?'

'Them.'

'Your family?'

'No.'

'So it's these boys, it's not something at home?'

'Why would it be at home? That's the only place I can relax.'

'Is it because of your height? I know it's difficult, I was the smallest in my class. But as you get older you learn to deal with it.'

'I was big when I was little,' I say. The man looks down at his pad and sort of nods.

'Sod this,' I say. 'Who are you? Why were you asking me about my sister? You leave her alone, don't talk to her.'

'Why not?'

'Don't you dare bother her,' I scream at him. He looks pretty scared.

'I have no intention of talking to her.'

I storm out of the room.

It's funny how you get used to things pretty quickly. I got used to my stomach pains in the morning. I'd be doubled up in bed when I woke up, and then again just before I left the house. But I could easily make sure no one saw me at those times. I could lie in the bath and listen to the immersion heater calm down after running all the hot water and I'd swear that I could hear their chanting. The quiet names, private phrases directed at me which I didn't understand and couldn't answer back. It's been seven days since I've had one of those things where I'm not really sure what's going on for a few seconds. I don't think those are anything abnormal. I am normal. I lie in the bath and try to relax.

The door flies open. Dad is standing there; the lock

has been ripped off with the force of him opening the door. He's out of breath.

'Are you okay?' he asks.

'Yeah,' I say.

'Then why didn't you answer? I've been calling you for ages, I was shouting. You've been in here for hours. I thought you'd drowned.'

I tell him I'm fine. He looks at the door: one of the hinges is buggered now. He brushes the little wood chips away from the hinge, looks embarrassed that he's damaged it. I can hear Mum calling him. He pulls the door closed as best he can. I close my eyes. Now it feels like they're here, with me; the same faces that are in the classroom; faces which I can't tell from each other.

8.

JOEL AND THE LOCUSTS

08.33, 51. The school gates.

Apparently they often ask after me at my last school. They want to know how I'm getting on. If I'm still winning those swimming races. Here, if you don't like the sports, and you aren't in a team, they still expect you to turn up and cheer at the games. I don't want to do that; I like being at home. And it's extra hours where I'm out in the open. I like basketball, and I can pass it well and run quite fast, but they just don't pick me. My penfriend sends me basketball magazines and stuff, so I know the plays and I'm really fit. But they're not interested. When I'm playing, they knock me over. The teacher doesn't say anything because he thinks those boys are so great. And I still haven't got used to this school going right up to eighteen years old – there are grown-up women everywhere, they don't look like they should be at school. They've got really long hair and they wear make-up and go out with ugly, hairy rugby players and walk like they should be somewhere else. I don't exactly know where.

08.50, 42. Guess-what-Joel.

I'm sitting in our Monday morning chapel. We used to
have assembly on Monday but since the holidays they've
moved it so we have chapel. One of the teachers reads
out a bit of the Bible, or one of the pupils does something.
I sit in row seven. I can hear my name being called from
behind me; they want me to look round but I don't. Then
one taps on my shoulder so I give in and when I do turn
round they just say, 'What?'

Joel is always late, but has a story every morning. I watch
him walk into chapel and he comes and sits by me as usual.
He's just joined the school, in the middle of the year, in
the middle of the service. That's the sort of thing he does.
There was a seat next to me so he put himself there on
the first day. He spoke to me, for no reason.

'Guess what, Marlow?' he now says every morning.
Usually he starts to tell me a story about some sixth form
girl he'd got off with, which I can't tell anyone about. These
stories are so amazing I can almost ignore what people are
saying behind me. Joel doesn't even notice that, behind us,
they're making gay sounds like I want to screw him, just
because I'm talking to him. What he's talking about all
sounds so exotic: Samantha, Kate, Debbie. They're like
the names of places in the Bible, places you have to travel
across hot deserts and fight battles in order to get to. Lands
which few people could have known about.

The people who used to be my friends, the people who
broke my watch, don't like Joel as he doesn't care what
they think of him. The best they can do is coming up to
me and saying, 'Marlow, guess what? Guess what? My

90

name's Joel. Guess what?' Or 'Oh Joel, I want to suck you.' I don't care. I think it's because I was pleased I had a friend and it was someone they couldn't control. Joel was beyond criticism. Joel didn't even notice them. He came from a world where long hair was normal, where he'd wear his Slayer T-shirt under his school shirt and when they told him to take it off he'd refuse. He smoked, but not because it was cool. He drank some American whiskey called Daniel's and he was wicked. I'd seen Joel and admired his long hair and the Metallica badge on his bag. Marty was cool too, but Joel was here, in the thick of it. I ended up next to him in biology on his first day, there was a spare seat next to me as usual, and I saw *Slayer* written on his folder.

'Oh, you like Slayer?' I'd asked him.

'What do you know about Slayer?' he'd asked, gruffly.

'I like them.'

'No you don't.'

'I do.'

'Do you?'

'Yes.'

'Oh, cool.'

'I'm going to see them play at the weekend,' I'd said.

'No you're not,' he'd laughed at me. It was the only time he ever did.

'I am.'

'No you aren't.'

'I am.'

'Are you?'

'Yes.'

'That's cool' he'd said, unimpressed. 'I saw them at Donnington.'

'You've been to Donnington?'

'Loads of times. My stepmother used to take me. She wants to screw the singer in Aerosmith.' From then on, we had something to talk about. I had met Joel and my friends hated it.

'Why d'you keep calling them your friends?' Joel says, as we walk out of chapel. 'They aren't your friends; they hate your guts. And you don't like them either. Check this out.' He shows me a passport photo of some girl who he'd got off with the night before. Then he hands me some tapes.

'You wanna get into this stuff. Thrash is old. This is what's really cool.' I look at the cover. *Bedtime for Democracy* by the Dead Kennedys.

'I've heard of them. Hasn't this one just come out?'

'Yeah. And I should get a dictionary and check out their lyrics. Then say some of them to those CCF cunts. Why d'you do that, anyway?'

'I thought you were supposed to,' I say. He takes the tape from me and opens up the lyric sheet. He points to a song called "Macho Insecurity".

'Read this,' he says. I do so, occasionally looking up the odd word in my pocket dictionary. I realise I'm reading something by the *other* person who must feel the same as me. I always thought it was just me. And every morning, during chapel, we talk about what Jello Biafra sings about. Then when we walk out, Joel walks with me, nodding to different girls, saying to me, 'kissed her, kissed her, kissed her.' It was the way he said 'kissed' which made it seem so classic. No one used the word *kissed*. He didn't need to make some stupid word up.

11.08, 26. Chemistry with Saccy.

Lieutenant Hedges also teaches chemistry. He sits at the front of the lab at a large wooden desk which is raised off the ground. He has a mug on the desk at all times. The liquid in the mug is clear and he's always going into his office to fill it up. He runs through an experiment:

'Now you add this to the boiling solution. Be careful you don't wobble as it mixes violently.' He pours one liquid on top of another. He has the shakes so badly that it starts to fizz and froth and comes out of the top of the boiling tube. He lets go of it and it smashes in the marble sink cut into his desk. 'Now, what happened there?' he asks the class.

'You shook it,' someone says.

'That's right. I did that on purpose to show you what happens. Carry on,' he waves, motioning for us to do our own version of the experiments as he runs for his office door. Most of the class get on with the experiment. I sit with Joel and read *Kerrang!* as they walk past us and make comments. Joel pays no attention, only looking up when the bell goes, to watch a girl blow him a kiss as she walks past. He smiles at her. Then one of the idiots that was making comments walks past us for the hundredth time that hour and says something about me and Joel, and without looking away from his magazine Joel reaches out quickly, grabs the boy's tie, and yanks it so the kid's face is flat on the table.

'Stop disturbing me,' Joel says, quietly, still in the middle of an article about Samhain. The kid grunts, his nose squashed against the table, his mates are laughing at him. Joel isn't even looking at him.

'Okay?' Joel says.

'Yeah,' the kid says. Joel lets him go.

'Who are you going to see Slayer with?' Joel says without missing a beat.

'A couple of friends.'

'Not these locusts?'

'No. Friends from home.'

12.21, 48. French.

The French teacher has a way of over-pronouncing everything, even if he's speaking in English. He asks us if we have any pets in French. We go round the class, but another teacher comes into the room and says the over-pronouncer is needed over at the staffroom. He says something about being grown up and being expected to get on with work quietly while he's gone. He walks out of the room. Sniggering starts. Someone comes up behind me and picks up my ruler and throws it at the window. It hits the pane, bounces off, and falls onto the floor.

'Go and get it then,' one of them says. In my mind I'm doing a little calculation about whether I really need the ruler and how much it cost and that I don't have maths today so I won't need it and that it was a crap one anyway so I'll just leave it there. Then someone picks up my fountain pen and my pencil case and chucks them both over towards the window. I sit there. I find a pen in my pocket and carry on writing, doing the exercise we were set.

'Go and pick your stuff up,' another says.

'Go on.'

'Pick it up, messy bastard.'

'Look, he's so keen to do his work!'

One of them gets up and picks up my pencil case off the floor. I move out of my chair and pick up my ruler and fountain pen. The boy who has my pencil case goes back to his desk, and looks through it. He starts taking pens and pencils out of it and throwing them individually, around the room. I run around the room picking them up. One of them says something about Mum, something about sex. Then another says that they saw my dad the other day and he looked like a tramp and they had heard he got the sack from his job for being pissed the whole time. Then one of them who I used to really know well does an impression of Cress. Then they say more things about my sister and how they want to screw her. It's like the opposite of the cinema – I'm looking at the audience and they're doing all the entertaining. I'm stuck there on the screen; I can't move and again all their faces merge and their voices overlap and people – Mum, Dad and Cress – are all mentioned along with the type of squash racket I have and how short I am and that my voice has not broken and how I've never got off with anyone and *I still can't move* and all of what they're saying about me is not being shouted. They're talking, it's clever what they're saying, it's not just insults. These are jokes, in-jokes which they've built up over time, and they're all coming out. A slow destruction of a personality – that's what was in those lyrics I read. They do this so that none of them will be the victim. They do this until the person is just like bits spilled from an empty pencil case all over the floor. They don't stop: the way I speak, the way I spend a lot of time by myself, the magazines I read, the colour of my blazer, the colour of my socks, the kind of gel in my hair, my gay shoes. But this isn't all happening now, this is the accumulation of hours of insults, hours of relentless knocks. This is a mental list which my head has kept hold of. They actually just said a few words in this French lesson, but that was the trigger. This is me letting go of all the things I've heard them say over the last months; I'm letting them go in one shot. My family, my hair, our car, my size. Everything is in there. The boys in front of me have been silent for a while. This is just me.

'SIT DOWN!' the teacher says. There's silence in the class. There's been silence for ages. I have all my pens in my hand and the class are looking at me with weird expressions on their faces. I think they stopped saying things to me a while ago. I go to sit down. As I pull my chair out I feel very dizzy. When I sit down I can feel my head sway. The teacher asks me a question about why I was standing up when he had said to get on with our work and says that I've got a detention and I'm trying to think where the detention hall is and how I'll miss my concert, and then his words trail off and I think I'm back standing by the window. I'm not too sure. When I wake up I'm lying in my own sick, on the table. Sick has gone all over my pens. My head aches and I can't lift it off the desk. I can't hear what anyone is saying to me. The white of Matron's uniform makes me feel even more sick. She helps me out of the room. As she takes me over to the medical office, Joel walks past.

'All right Marlow?' he says, looking worried.

14.56, 19. Biology.

Joel will be sitting in biology. People will be messing around, some will be working. He'll be doing no work, he'll be drawing album covers on his file. No one will say anything to him. And when he walks out of the lesson he'll run up to some girl that all the rugby players like and just start chatting to her. They'll leave him alone. Leave me alone.

15.31, 16. Home.

It's probably just a bug. Mum says the teacher came in and found me standing by the window for no reason and everyone was getting on with their work. When I came to sit down I was sick.

'I think it's a nasty bug,' she says. She came and picked me up from school. When Dad gets home he comes into my room. He smells of petrol and grease.

It's a nice smell, a strong, tough smell. He sits on the end of the bed and tells me about his day. Then Mum comes in and tells him to get off the bed as he's covered in grease. Then Cress comes in. She brings a new tape she's just got and says I can borrow it, but only until I'm better.

'What's the matter?' she says. She looks so healthy.

'I don't know.'

18.00, 36. Marty phones.

'Come over to Richie's,' Marty says. 'We're roller skating in his kitchen, his mum is away and his sister is upstairs with her boyfriend.'

'No thanks.'

'Eh?' he says. I hear a high-pitched squawk and then some laughing.

'What was that?' I ask.

'Richie's chasing the cat around the house on skates, I think he's just run over it.'

I hear Richie's voice. 'I'll never give in, jungle beast!'

'Why aren't you coming over?' Marty says.

'I don't feel like it.'

'You missed skating last week as well.'

'I've got to go, Marty.'

I go up and lie on my bed. Once the stomach pains go I manage to get to sleep.

07:15, 34. Morning.

'Are you well enough to go in?'

'No, I don't think so,' I lie.

'You don't want to go making yourself worse,' Mum says and calls Aldridge and tells him that I'll be away today but maybe back tomorrow.

'I've got to go now, but Dad isn't leaving until nine. He'll come in and see you before he goes.'

I lie in bed. Mum goes out. An hour or so later Dad walks in.

'You okay?'

'Not really.'

'Your sister's ill as well.'

'Really? She was all right last night.'

Dad shrugs. 'You've got the number for me today. I'll give you a ring at lunch-time. You be all right here?'

'Yeah.'

He leaves the room. I lie there and listen to him start the car up; he has a special ordered way of doing it to get it started. Then he drives off. Ten seconds later Cress comes in.

'Hello!'

'You're not ill. How did you pull that one?'

'I told Dad I was feeling ill, and he believed me.' She clicks her finger above her head like she's magic, and smiles. 'So we can do something today.'

'I'm actually ill. I feel like shit.'

'What's going on, Marlow?' she says, sitting on the edge of the bed.

99

'Stop prying into my life, will you? It's all right for you.'

'What is?'

'Nothing. You wouldn't understand. Just get off the bed.'

'*Sorry,*' she says, and buggers off. The phone rings, but Cress doesn't answer it. If she's downstairs she might get it. But it keeps ringing. I walk onto the little landing, past Cress's room – where is she? – and into Mum and Dad's room and pick it up. I can hear laughing, sounds like someone is going to be sick. I put the phone down. It rings again: the same sounds. I wheel the TV into my room and stick it on and get back into bed. If I lie on my side at an angle I can watch it and keep the stomach pains away. I lie there for three or four hours, and cry a bit, but not too much. Cress comes in with some soup at midday. She passes it to me. Then she lies on top of the duvet, next to me, and falls asleep. She's very warm and soon I fall asleep as well. When I wake she's not there, but Mum is in the room, holding bags of shopping.

'You know that girl who came round with Cress's friend? Peri,' she says.

'Eh?' I say, half asleep.

'I bumped into her mother in the shops and she says Peri's ill and at home. Apparently she's been ill for weeks. Has anyone at your school got this thing? It's like glandular fever but it has a different name. I can't remember.'

'Maybe I've got it.'

'No, you haven't got a temperature. You'll be fine in a day or so.'

She hands me an orange from her shopping bags.

'Well, I've got to unload this lot. This is the girl's number if you want. She's not contagious to be in the same room with any more. Maybe you could take Cress over to see her. All cheer each other up.'

I've never phoned a girl before. I've only seen her a few times. I panic for a second, then I just dial Peri's number and as it rings it feels like I'm free-falling.

9.

THE KISSING DISEASE

'Hello?'

'It's Marlow.'

'Hello Marlow,' Peri says. It sounds a bit weird the way she says it. 'How're you?'

'I'm ill, like you.'

'I'm *really* ill.'

'What's the matter with you?'

'I've got something fever.'

'What's that?'

'Like glandular fever, gives you a temperature and you can't swallow. What's your problem?'

'I just don't feel well.'

'What's wrong?'

'I don't know,' I say, avoiding her question. There's silence for a second. I look around my room, can't think of anything to say.

'Well, bye Peri,' I say and put the phone down. I close my eyes and pull the duvet over my head.

An hour later the phone rings.

'It's me.'

'Who?' I ask.

'Me, you idiot,' Peri says. 'My mum was in the room when you phoned. She's gone out now. Hopefully, she won't ever come back, bitch. I feel fuckin' shit. Bastard fucking crap shit. And you?'

I'd never heard a girl swear with such freedom. I liked it.

'I just feel ill.'

'Right, Marlow, here's what we're gonna do. Either you're gonna tell me what's wrong with you or I'm gonna hang the phone up 'cos you're boring me. What's it going to be?'

Jesus, what is this girl like?

'I'll tell you if I see you. Mum wants me to bring Cress over to see you.'

'Fuck that. Why don't you sneak over here tomorrow by yourself. Get on your bike or something and come over. That's if you're not too *ill*,' she laughs, 'with your sore throat or whatever. My mother will be out. D'you want to come?'

'Um . . .'

'Fine. Don't bother then.' She hangs the phone up. She does things too quickly for me. I call her number.

'What?!' comes the answer.

'I'm a bit slow at the moment, Peri,' I say.

'Oh my God, listen to you Marlow, you little poppet. I bet you're getting murdered at that corporate shit school.'

'I'll come over tomorrow and see you.'

'You will,' she confirms.

'See you then,' I say.

'So unusual,' she laughs, a little.

Peri's house is nice. There's lots of oak panels – that's

what she tells me, I'm not interested in houses – and big rooms. Peri opens the door for me. She's wearing one of those towelling dressing gowns and her hair is all tied up at the back. Her green eyes look red and her face is swollen.

'Do I look that bad?' she says.

'Yes.'

She looks shocked. 'Well, you're honest, aren't you.'

I go into her bedroom and sit on the bed while she gets under the covers.

'Will your mum mind me being here?' I ask.

'Yes, she'll go apeshit. But fuck it. Now, tell me why you're off school.'

'Well, I had a um . . .'

'What? Piece of chewing gum?' She wriggles around and finds the remote control, turns the TV down. I look around the room: the walls are covered with posters of singers and people wearing black, looking pissed off. There are lots of records on the floor, some in their cases and some out. Black T-shirts and skirts and shoes are also scattered around.

'I kind of blacked out, I think.'

'That is *cool*,' she says. 'That is cool. Did you see devils or anything?'

'I don't remember what I saw.'

She sees me looking around the room. 'You like it? I'm into all this wicked music that only I like. Have you heard of the Misfits?'

'Glenn Danzig,' I say.

'Fuck me, how does someone like you know that?'

'I'm into them.'

'No you're not.'

'I am.'

Why does no one ever believe me?

'Shit. Well, I borrowed these, but I'm not giving them back. I bet you don't know many girls who like this stuff?'

I shrug.

'How's that school?' she asks. I go quiet, don't say anything. It feels like my first day every day, but I've been there a year and a half. I don't want to say that to her.

'What's the matter?' she says, softly. 'Are those public school fuckers being bastards.'

'They're all right.'

'What's going on? If you could see your face, you look more ill than me.'

'But you've got a proper disease,' I say.

'I have,' she says, 'but I've got *so* much more. Have you?'

All Peri can drink is hot lemon with honey in it, so I make her one of those. I make me one, too. It makes me feel better. She has two paracetamol and I have a couple as well. We switch on the TV and watch a thing about Ronald Reagan in court. It gets boring as all he says is, 'I don't recall.' We switch it off.

'Marlow, I've got an idea.'

'What?'

'D'you want some more time off school?'

'I don't know.'

'Of course you fuckin' do, you hate it and you hate those bastards.'

'I hate those bastards,' I say, repeating her back to herself.

'Good. Well, I was thinking, you don't seem to talk much, you wouldn't be too much trouble, we could hang around together if we were both off school.'

'But I'm going back tomorrow.'

'But I've got a plan. You can get this glandular fever thing. Do you know what its nickname is?'

'Glandi?'

'No. It's the Kissing Disease. It gets passed on through gob.'

'Gob?'

'So, you could get it, too,' she says excitedly.

'How would I get it?'

'You'd have to have some of my gob.'

'That's disgusting.'

The next day I'm back at school. Voices say the same things, and each time I think I know what they're saying, they change it to something new, like a mutating virus which is always one step ahead of the cure. Mum picks me up as usual, asks me how my day was, and I lie as usual. That evening, as I'm dozing off, my dad comes in and sits on the end of the bed. He doesn't put the light on and he whispers. I can smell the comforting garage smell on him.

'Marlow, are you awake?'

'Yes.'

'Marlow, are you unhappy at school?'

'Yes.'

'What shall we do about it?'

'I don't know.'

'I'll try to be around more now . . . if you want to talk to me you can. You know that?'

'Yeah,' I say. He gets up from our whispered conversation, holds his hand on my head for a solid moment and it feels peaceful. I sleep better than I have for a year. I wake up in the morning and feel great. At school it's worse than ever. Drip, drip, drip, their words just dent me, bit by bit, by bit. I get home and phone Peri.

'What d'you want?' she asks.

'Can I come over?' I ask.

'Why?' she says.

'Just can I?'

She says yes, even though her parents are there.

I say hello to them as I walk in, but they're very busy tidying up some little green twigs and buds in a little bowl on the table. There are bits of folded white paper and matches everywhere. Peri's mother must be ill as well, as she sniffs a lot. Maybe she has the same thing as Peri. They don't seem to mind me going into her room which is a bit weird, but then Peri is ill so maybe that changes those kind of rules. She's lying in bed, looking a lot better.

'You look nice, Peri,' I say.

'Really?' she says, her whole face lights up. 'And to what do I owe this visit?'

'I've decided,' I say.

'Decided what?'

'I want the kissing disease.'

'You do? Okay then. You know what it means?'

108

'Does it mean we can see each other and chat and things?' It feels like I've rediscovered talking.

'Well, yeah. I mean, I'll listen to you. And we can both listen to the Misfits.' She leans over and puts the needle onto a record on the turntable. *'This is Hatebreeders, 1, 2, 3, 4 . . .'* Glenn shouts, seconds before the fleet of chugging guitars burst out of the speakers. I look at Peri.

'Well, I could spit into your hand and you could lick it or something, but you need to get it really into your gums and stuff to get infected. Don't *wince* when I say that, Marlow, this is one of the coolest ideas ever.'

'Yes,' I say.

'So come here and we'll kiss and then you've got a better chance of getting it.'

'And I can come over and see you.'

'Yes, although for some of the time you'll be too ill to move or swallow, and two per cent of people who get it, die.'

'Okay,' I say. I move towards her. She shuffles in her bed. We edge towards each other. I look at her lips, getting closer to me, to my first kiss. The door opens.

'How are things in here?' Peri's mother says, as we both move away from each other.

'Fine,' I say. Peri gives her mother a look which says, 'Get out!' Glenn Danzig calls the audience a bunch of cocksuckers. Peri's mum sighs and goes to leave. *'Move on up here a little bit, so we can see yer faces, yeah . . . we think we know ya, we ain't that scary,'* Glenn growls. I watch her mother close the door and I turn back round. As I do, Peri's mouth is on mine, her lips are sliding around on mine. She's moving her mouth like she's a goldfish trying to get air – that's what real kissing is – so I do the same. We do that for a while and it's hot and Peri is lush and my dick feels mad and we just keep on doing it and I can't believe it, have you ever done this? It's weird and I can't describe it and *Oh my God* I can feel her tongue in my mouth, swirling around . . . shit, this is mental and I now put my tongue back in her mouth and we keep doing it and doing it. My dick is totally hard, too. How embarrassing. Finally we stop.

'That should do it,' Peri says.

I don't say anything.

'How was it?'

'Nice.'

'Want to do it again, just to be sure?'

'Think so.'

I go to school the next morning. I can't stop thinking about her. I keep waiting to feel ill, but nothing. Nothing happens. I will it on, I keep thinking I'm feeling bad, but nothing. Then on Saturday we're forced to support the rugby team. I stand on the sideline in the cold rain and pretend to care. I have to miss Mum's birthday. I can hear others chant for the team to win, and I can hear them chant things about me. I decide to leave, I don't care what happens, hopefully I'll get run over. As I walk down the little path that links the rugby field to the school, rain gets down my neck, and I step in a puddle. A stone lands in the puddle, thrown by someone behind me. It splashes. I can feel the water seep into my shoes. I go to bed early that night. When I wake up on Sunday my throat feels a bit sore and I say I'm too ill to go to church. Mum says it was all that standing around in the rain. They get back late because Cress wanted to buy a magazine and only one shop was open. Mum is still cursing when she walks into my room and wakes me up. I'm lying in a pool of sweat. Mum takes my temperature and calls a doctor, who comes round to take a blood test!

'Haven't seen you since you were a baby,' says the doctor. 'He looks like you, doesn't he?' she says to Mum. 'What a strong family resemblance.' She starts getting needles out. She catches me looking, so she carries on talking. 'Yes, very strong.'

'D'you think?' Mum says, unsure. 'I don't know.'

'You look like your mum with your dark hair,' she says. Cress walks into the room. 'And you look like your dad,' she says.

'I sometimes think we all look different,' Mum says. 'Just a funny mixture.' Cress stands in the doorway, and the conversation bounces around.

'There, all done,' the doctor says. I look down and there's a tiny plaster on my arm, where she took the blood.

'That was amazing.' I say. The doctor smiles.

I don't sleep very well overnight, and when it comes to time for school I know I'm not up to it. I'm sweating like hell, it's disgusting. Someone from the surgery rings with the results.

'Marlow, I'm afraid she thinks you've got gland-ular fever.'

I look at her.

'Why're you smiling?' she asks.

'I've got glandular fever?' I say.

'That's brilliant!' Peri says, as soon as I get a chance to phone her. 'I knew we could do it! We've beaten them,' she says.

'Who've we beaten?'

'The school and our parents, the government. We beat them all just with a kiss.' Peri is a poet and now I love her. Over the next few days I call her whenever my parents are out. We talk about music, what I've read in *Kerrang!* that week, what's on telly.

'What video are you watching today? Not more horror?' she asks.

'Yeah, this man has thousands of needles sticking in his head.'

'That's disgusting. How're you feeling?'

'Feeling really bad.'

'Yeyyyy!' she shrieks. 'Cramps?'

'Yes.'

'Temperature?'

'Well over a hundred!' We rejoice.

'Have you got the sore throat?'

'I can't even swallow!' I gush.

'We did it!' she says. 'So what's going on in the film now?'

'They've ripped his face off with fish hooks.'

'Echh!' she screams. 'Stop!' Brief pause, 'What does it look like?'

A week into the disease I can't even eat anything apart from soup. I start to lose weight. For a few days I'm too ill to speak to Peri on the phone. The doctor comes over again as Mum is worried – there are a few strains of this which are supposed to be dangerous! But she says mine is perfectly normal.

'How would he have got it?' Mum asks while the doctor packs up her things in my room.

'Well,' she says, smiling. 'I'm sure you remember being a teenager, Mrs Walker? Kissing behind the bike sheds.'

'Well, Marlow hasn't been kissing anyone,' she says.

'It must have been an immaculate infection, then,' the doctor says, and winks at me so Mum can't see.

'The last thing we need in this house is more kissing,' Mum says, glaring at Cress, who's loitering by the door again. Cress got caught kissing a boy at school last week. She got into trouble.

'That's the last thing we need in this family.'

My glands are so swollen and my throat is so inflamed that I can't actually speak for four days. I'm really glad when I get my voice back and Peri and I start speaking again. What about this for a disease!

'Where the hell have you been?' she asks.

'I couldn't speak,' I say.

'Excellent. I had that. You know what I was thinking?' she says.

'What?'

'Well, I hope we're both at the same stage of the illness, you know, so we both have the same time off school. I don't want to go back if I know you're having a great time at home,' she says.

'Great time? I can't stand up and last week I couldn't speak!' I say, but she isn't interested.

113

'Well, I think we should do it again. Y'know so we're both at the same stage. Just to make sure.'

'Just to make sure,' I say. *Just to make sure* are the finest words. We talk about a day when her parents are out and when I'll be well enough to go over to her house. That was one thing we hadn't really thought through. Just because you try and give yourself a disease doesn't mean you can turn it on and off at different times.

The day comes. My parents are out and I get out of bed. It's the first time I've walked for over three weeks. My body feels heavy, even though I've lost nearly a stone. My head feels wooden and solid, my back aches. I'm so dizzy I have to hold onto the wall as I walk around the house. It feels like there's more gravity than normal. I put on my clothes, which feel itchy on my skin. I walk outside and the cold air nearly knocks me over. I can feel myself sway, the dizziness nearly throws me onto the floor. I sit down on the ground by the garage for a second, get myself together. I stand back up, and slowly move around the garage to get my bike out. I start my journey to Peri's. I nearly ride straight into the hedge at one point – my balance isn't very good. But I keep thinking about kissing her again and I know it's worth it. When I get to her driveway neither of her parents' cars are there. I smile and speed up, but the driveway is gravel and I skid around and lose control of the bike. I fly over the handlebars, hit the ground and lie there for a second. I haul myself back up, and knock on the door but there's no answer. The door is open so I walk in. There's broken stuff in the kitchen, smashed plates. I walk through to her bedroom. She's in bed; she's crying.

'What's the matter?' I say. She jumps when she hears my voice.

'Oh, Marlow, I forgot you were coming over.'

'What's the matter?'

'I'm not well.'

'Me too. I feel so hot I think I might have a heart attack in a minute,' I gush.

'No, I mean I'm not well. Nothing to do with our disease.'

'You look pretty today.'

She looks down, wipes her eyes. 'Look, Marlow you're going to have to go. My parents are on their way back. A special doctor is coming here. I can't see you any more.'

'Shall I ring you tomorrow then?'

'No. I mean I can't see you *any more*. You'll have to go.'

I pedal the bike back to my house. I bet Peri just felt sick, I'll phone her tomorrow. I keep pedalling. It takes a lot longer on the way back and I have to keep stopping for a rest. When I get back, my parents go apeshit.

'What the hell were you doing out on your bike with a temperature? Why are your trousers ripped?' Mum shouts. I go to bed and sleep for twenty-four hours. When I wake up I think about phoning Peri but I know she'll phone me soon enough.

The next three weeks of the disease are boring. I start feeling a bit better and walk around a bit. Peri doesn't phone. I go out to the shops one time with Mum and don't feel too bad. Still, Peri doesn't phone. I ask Mum if she knows what's going on with Peri and her family.

She says she doesn't know her mum very well, she couldn't ask. So finally I phone. I phone a few times and sometimes there's no answer and other times her mum says Peri is away and one time she says she's changing schools.

Cress gets caught at school again; she was in the girls' toilets with a boy. Mum won't tell me the rest, and neither will she. Mum seems pretty worried, and she talks to the teacher on the phone quite often. Cress doesn't think she's doing anything wrong, if you ask me. I don't think she knows what she's doing. She always comes in after school, sits on my bed and talks crap about her day, about which boys she likes. But she never says anything about what she does with them. She talks on the phone with her friends a lot, but I can't hear from my room, and I'm too ill to stand by the door under Jesus.

Finally, after two months, the kissing disease gives up. I just imagined it would give up as soon as I stopped seeing Peri, because there was no point in having it if she wasn't there. It was a good friend and I'll miss it. The night before I start back at school I lie in bed and brace myself. I think about what they're all going to say. Then I stop thinking about it. I think about what I read in a rock mag last week. One of those singers, maybe it was Glenn? said, 'Fuck them, I don't care what those motherfuckers say. They can kiss my ass!' I think about all those motherfuckers waiting for me at school. It's all right for people like Glenn: his arms are the size of my legs. I make myself stop thinking about school. I think about Peri's warm lips, and breath and tongue and how hot it was kissing her, and how pretty she was, and our tongues twisting as I let her infect me.

5'4"

10.

LARRY WATCHES OVER ME

I waited for two years for Peri to phone. Her mother said she'd started at a new boarding school in the north of England. Why didn't she phone me herself? I missed her. School became a little better; we were doing our GCSEs so I wasn't really around too much. And people were busy with their work. Then on my birthday the whole of the world's stock markets went mental and everyone lost loads of money. I don't think the two events were linked. It was cool having your birthday called Black Monday.

The summer comes and so does the Saturday night ritual. Someone's parents away, a party at their house. This time it's Simon's party. His parents have an amazing house, really big. He likes all these bands that write songs about South Africa and Belfast. They play these songs in football arenas. I go along with Marty and Richie, and Joel comes from school. Joel tells me Marty is a total Kev, but I don't know what that means. I see one of the people from my class and they even say hello to me. They say my name. I drink some cider which I don't like, but it's nicer than beer. Richie is there with some girl, and he introduces me to someone called Carla. She has a bottle of Malibu in her hand and is drinking it very quickly. All evening she asks if we can be alone. I say to her, 'What for?' and then, when we *are* alone, she just kisses me, like that's supposed to explain.

I don't know what the hell is going on.

She kisses me again and then gives me a funny look as if I'm supposed to know what she means. What are girls on about? I take her behind a bush somewhere and sit on the ground. There are no lights, but the summer evening is still warm and it never gets completely dark. I kiss her and we roll around on the ground and into a pile of freshly cut grass which looks like it's been put there for a bonfire. The grass goes down the back of my neck and itches, like hair does when you've had a haircut. I can't believe how stupid flat tops are, now. Thank God I never had one.

'Are you concentrating, Michael?' Carla says.

'It's Marlow,' I say.

'And it's *Catherine*,' she says. We've both drunk a lot of cider. Kissing her feels boring compared to Peri. I think about that priest bloke from *The Thorn Birds*. Now he could really kiss. He'd kiss that Megan and you could really see he knew what he was doing. That was one Almighty kiss he gave her. Ha! And he was a priest, too. So I try all that stuff, moving my mouth all over the place and all she can do is stick her tongue in and out. This is my first official snog and I'm not enjoying it very much. I never told anyone about kissing Peri – it was something I thought about all the time but I classed it as different. Why was there one kiss that I remembered? Why would one be different, when all you're doing is the same thing. Even though it was just part of our experiment, to get the disease, it stayed with me.

122

We find our way into Simon's bedroom. He has loads of pictures of rock stars all over the walls and a bloody great giant Swatch. We go over to the bed and as I lie on top of Catherine I realise she's taller than me. She sits up on the bed – it's a single bed – and I look up and see a big picture of Larry Mullen looking down at me, drumsticks in hand. He looks like he's laughing at me. Larry isn't being any bloody help. I can hear people outside, chatting to each other and messing around. I'm praying someone will come and get me so I can get my lift home, or maybe I'm needed for something. Anything. That's what was so good about Father Ralph de Bricassart. He'd do some wicked snogging but he always had to leave early to go and have tea with the Pope and confess his sins. But no one comes.

I'm scared.

And not scared and intrigued, but terrified and I want to be at home with a cup of tea and some cereal and watch the Laurel and Hardy that I taped. She takes her jumper off. Underneath is a white bra. Her bra is full of her tits – I can't believe it! People seem so sad when they're naked if you don't really know them. I don't know what I was expecting, but I wasn't expecting that feeling somehow. She looks at me, she seems sort of helpless, like a seal. She says, 'My tits are too small, aren't they?' while I stare at them – the first ones I've ever seen in real life. I say, 'They aren't small,' just like I'm really knowledgeable. I know nothing. She takes her bra off and there they are, suspended without anything holding them. Real ones. She lies back on the bed. Jesus! Someone come in now! Someone rush in and say, 'Marlow! the hospital called, there's been an accident . . .' and I could jump off the bed and run out of the room like a hero. Maybe the Pope could phone and say I had to go to Rome, sharpish. I'd jump onto a horse and ride off into the distance. *Dear God*, get me out of this now and I promise I'll never go near another woman again. I'd give anything for someone to say that I had to keep an eye on Cress as she was trying to be Rapunzel again, tying long bits of string into her hair and leaning out the window, shouting at men below. Someone stop this.

But nothing.

I lean forward, my T-shirt presses against her body. There's more of that kissing and I stick my tongue right back at her to sort of say, 'Stop doing that!' but she just does it more. Then I remember *Top Gun*. Everything was silhouetted, with that blue light coming in the room. That was sex. Well, the moonlight is sort of casting a silhouette here. So I get up and draw the curtain a little, and sure enough, when I look in the mirror on the wall, we're silhouetted. So now I can get down to business. Maybe everything else will just happen naturally. I kiss her neck. She smells of lemon shampoo, perfume, hair spray, loads of sweet-scented make-up, Malibu, Coca-Cola, girl's skin. Girl's skin is the most alien and the nicest. It's so soft – the only thing which reminds me of kissing Peri. I wouldn't have minded lying there with my face in what's-her-name's neck but I think I should do something. I've got a wicked boner! She tries to put her hands down my trousers! Mad! Luckily I move because I might spunk or something. Can you imagine spunking in front of someone else? How embarrassing! I kiss her on the chest and then peck at her left tit, and no one dies. I kiss the right one and neither the hand of God nor Larry Mullen strikes me down. Perhaps Larry approves. I kiss her near her stomach button, but not *in* it, because that would be disgusting. I sit up on the bed, job completed. The big giant Swatch hanging on the wall says it's late. I think I've done a pretty good job. One woman satisfied.

She grabs me and pulls me back towards her.

The thing is, if I took my pants off, she'd see my dick. I'd be so embarrassed; I'd never be able to do anything. That's why I prefer magazines, you can do it in private. That's the main problem with Catherine: she's so, so *3D*. She unbuttons her jeans. Jesus! She slides them off and under she has on knicker things which match the pattern of the bra she had on. There's so much *to* girls, isn't there? So many things going on, you don't know where to start, where to look first. She asks me again if her boobs are too small. I feel like telling her, 'I've no idea and I don't care.' Her tits are lush. I kiss her on her mouth and she kind of pushes me onto her tits again. So I go through the routine again like an old pro. Kissed them both twice! Don't touch her nipples though, because that would be disgusting. Then I get down to her belly button again and kiss below it and there seems to be more skin, more space than I imagined there would be. And she starts making these stupid sounds. God knows what the hell they're supposed to mean. But at least we're silhouetted and I can't see bloody Larry from this angle.

125

I still don't really need to shave so my smooth face rubs against her stomach which is even smoother. She makes some more noises as I keep on going.

I'm quite enjoying myself now. I remember Tom Cruise doing this: moving down a girl's body slowly. They seem to like that, don't they? So I keep going and suddenly I feel something really coarse against my face. I lift my head a bit and her pants aren't there! She's taken them off somehow. How'd she do that? My face is being scraped by all this hair between her legs. Really loads of it – thick hair everywhere in a triangle and I can smell something like her skin only sort of stronger. I've got the feeling of being outdoors. I don't know why that is.

I hear people coming up the stairs. Thank God! *Top Gun* kind of stopped at this point because they had to do a flying exercise the next morning and I was running out of ideas. I jump up and throw her jumper and jeans at her. I run to the door but Richie and everyone bounce in. I look behind me but she's sitting on the bed, with her jeans and her top on already! She's fast. She walks out slowly and winks at me as she passes. They all cheer. I don't tell them what happened so of course they all think it was something mega. As I go to leave the party, to get picked up, I pass Catherine or whatever her name is.

'It's my tits, isn't it? They're too small,' she whispers.

'They're not. It was just people were coming up the stairs. I heard them.'

'So, it's not my tits?'

'No. They were about to burst into the room. I didn't want you to be embarrassed.' I look at her, and at her chest, 'They're . . . nice,' I say.

126

'Really?' Her face lights up. She hugs me and kisses me, this time without any of that stupid tongue crap. She walks off looking happy and starts chatting excitedly with her friends. So, it turns out, understanding girls is easy.

11.

MUGGSY GETS DRAFTED

Their voices solidify, freezing over me, strangling me so I can't breathe, and then slowly and silently creep around my body, encasing me in insults and icicles that will have to be cracked through by some poor girlfriend – if I ever get one – or some overpaid therapist who will only be disappointed with me as a case study.

My sixteenth birthday is approaching. It turns out the brief gap, when they left me alone, was because we were on study leave. No one was *around* to say or do anything. I'd just forgotten again, like I do every evening, thinking tomorrow will be better.

I was talking to Dad last night. He was teaching me to punch. Mum came in and went a bit mad – said he was inciting violence. He said that self-defence was better than no defence at all. Dad is happier now than he used to be. Since he finished his job he's started talking to me and to Cress. Mum looks 'wired' all the time. My pen pal Garry in America always uses that word. I like it. Garry is short, too. That's what we write about. It sounds even worse at an American school. We send each other stuff almost every week. He likes British music, and we both like basketball. He sends me this whole article on Muggsy Bogues. He's 5'3" and just got into the NBA. The smallest player ever! I stick it up on my wall. At school, they still don't let me play basketball.

Mum has this worried look on her face, and she's really strict with Cress since her things with those boys. She and Dad don't seem to like each other any more. When I go to hug her, she feels brittle. One thing that hasn't changed is that she's still trying to get me into religion like you wouldn't believe. I still can't handle it. Jesus died for my sins. *My* sins? That's insane – all I've done is stay up late when I said I was going to bed, buy some Slayer records, look at the magazines that Danny gets, and kiss Catherine. If Jesus died for just that, when I really do something wrong it's going to be a bloodbath.

I'm lying to you. I'll admit it. There was another party the week after that one when I was under Larry's gaze. This was a few months back. I got more into the drinking and had a two litre bottle of cider. Catherine was there again and we ended up by a hedge at the bottom of the garden. She got her hand down my trousers this time and wasn't going to give up. I did like it; I'll have to admit that. And I'm starting to think women are pretty nice after all, even if they do smell weird and have all kinds of mad curves everywhere and you never understand what the hell they're on about. I put my hand down her trousers as well. I won't even start about that. My fingers were wet by the end. I don't know what I was expecting but that was pretty mad. That was as far as I wanted to go, at that time.

Joel has done everything. And he tells me all about it. During chapel he tells me really graphic stories about what he did at the weekend and what girls are like when they *really* get going. I realise that I hadn't got Catherine going as much as I'd thought. Joel says they make all kinds of loud noises and you think they're gonna lose it but it's just them enjoying it. I'm glad he told me, or I'd be there thinking I'd killed her. I'm still not as into it as Joel. Or Prince. Everyone loves his new one. Thing is, when Prince says, 'C*ruuu*shaahlll . . . think I wantcha!' it sounds pretty cool. When I say crucial, it doesn't sound so good.

Sometimes I don't make it to chapel, I just hide in the wardrobe in one of the rooms in the classroom blocks. Sometimes the teacher finds me, which is pretty embarrassing. But some of the others think it's pretty cool, doing that. I don't know why. I'm just about to climb into the wardrobe for another thirty minutes of sitting in the dark, alone, doing nothing, when I hear Aldridge come down the stairs above me. I know I can't get in the damn thing in time so I leg it and pretend I'm on my way to chapel. As I run down the smooth stone stairs, with his footsteps not far behind me, I trip and fall. I fall backwards and bump down about twenty stairs. I end up at the bottom in a heap.

'Have you hurt yourself?' Aldridge asks, coming round the corner.

'Yes,' I groan. I fell for my sins. I get home and have to tell Mum what happened. Dad thinks it's funny, hiding in the bloody wardrobe to avoid religion. What's funny about that?

For the next few days I have really bad headaches and my neck hurts like hell. Mum phones one of her posh

131

friends and tells me I have to go to an osteopath. This is some person who bends you in half to make you better. It means I get a day off school as he only works in the daytime. For some reason I can't get an appointment for ages. Dad gets cross and says he'll find a different osteopath. He and Mum fight.

When I walk in the osteopath asks me to take my top off and stand, facing away from him. I do that and he traces a finger down my spine.

'You've really got some curvature here; it's quite serious,' he says. All I can imagine is a surgeon cutting my back open, blood everywhere, holding my spine in his hand against the light – like a fisherman does when he's landed a bloody great trout – and straightening it with his bare hands before putting it back in.

'Do I have to have an operation?' I ask him. He laughs.

'No, but you'll need a series of treatments. Probably six to start with, and then we'll take it from there.' He gets out his notepad and starts writing things down. He asks me about my weight, my height and my age, how big my family are. I hang, almost upside down, on this thing that looks like a padded see-saw, while he talks and asks me questions. He has a nice voice and is very kind to me. He saw Prince play live! He said he had to hold onto his girlfriend. Perhaps she gets lost easily. Mum comes to pick me up and he invites her into the consulting room.

'It's just as well you came in now. There's a curve in his spine that's been there a lot longer than, when did you say you fell?'

'Last week,' I say.

'Well, this has been here for some time. I don't think the fall did much, apart from strain the muscles around your neck,' he says to me. 'That's where these headaches are coming from. I don't think that's really anything to worry about. How old are you, again?'

'I was sixteen a few weeks ago,' I say.

'So there's nothing to worry about then,' Mum says. The osteopath ignores her and talks to me. He has large forearms which are very evenly suntanned.

'Well, I would say you'll grow until you're twenty. You can usually get a pretty good guess at how tall someone will be after a good examination and a review of the family. With your son, it doesn't tally, Mrs Walker,' he says.

'What do you mean?' she says.

'I mean his bones, particularly in his back are . . . look, imagine a flower has been planted at the wrong angle. Even if it grows towards the sunlight it'll never be as big as it could be, because it's fighting gravity and going in the wrong direction. The same has happened with your son. Didn't you think it was strange that he was so small and all the rest of the family were tall?'

'We thought that was just Marlow.'

'Well,' he says, a little angry if you ask me, 'he needs treatment, starting tomorrow and then once a week for six weeks. Then possibly more. Also I'd like the head osteopath here to look at him, *with your permission*,' he adds, after a pause. 'My guess is that the treatment will loosen up the spine and allow it to grow. Now, this is dangerous in itself as he may grow too quickly and that can also cause problems.'

My mother's face is white. You should see it. Someone has finally shut her up.

'Into his twenties he'll need to be vigilant as well. He still won't be out of the danger area. There is a kind of arthritis which strikes in the early twenties in cases like these.'

'I don't know what to say,' she says. 'Are you sure you aren't putting ideas into his head?'

'No, I'm not.'

'Can it affect his, you know, personality and emotions . . . moving his bones around so much?' she asks.

'I seriously doubt it – unless you count growing to a full height as a problem.'

'Oh,' Mum says.

We get in the car and I wait to be tall. When I get back to school, they ask me if it's true I have to have a major operation or I won't walk again. I think, what the hell, and say that it's true. They seem really interested in all that. A few of them still say things to me, nasty things. But a couple of the others, my older friends, start talking to me again. They act like nothing ever happened. This other guy, Neil, starts getting all the same shit from them. Neil's dad drinks a lot. I watch them as they lay into him and make up songs and stuff. I don't join in with them.

Joel comes and sits by me in biology. 'You're not chatting with those cunts, are you?'

'Well, a couple of them are all right,' I say.

'No they aren't. Have you seen the way they're laying into Neil.'

'But Neil likes Abba.'

'It doesn't matter. Neil's a dick but he deserves to be left alone. Can't you see what they're doing?'

'No.'

'They've found someone else.'

School passes through another term. My six osteopath visits turn into twelve. My GP gets involved – my wicked osteopath is accusing everyone he can find, Mum, Dad, my doctor, of neglecting me. How cool! He's really nice and we talk about girls and stuff. He's about thirty I reckon. I hope I'm like him.

It gets towards the end of term and another careers day. When I wake up I can't speak. Mum thinks I'm having one of my turns, but I'm not. After two cups of tea I get my voice back. And my voice is someone else's. My osteopath laughs like hell when I go back with my new voice. He seems really pleased. He says I won't be able to sing 'Kiss' like Prince does anymore. My back feels better and I stop getting headaches. He says it's starting to straighten nicely. It's responding to the treatment. Sometimes, when he's finished, he sticks a funny, warm metal box under a pillow and puts it on my back, lets it work the magic as I grow up to the sky. He tells me all kinds of things I should be doing: eating broccoli, pasta, drinking lots of water, taking vitamins. I do what he says.

'You won't need such regular treatments soon. Things are progressing nicely.'

135

'Oh.'

'What's that matter?'

'No, nothing.'

'If you want to come round and just chat, you can still do that . . .'

'That'd be cool,' I say. He's really curt with Mum when she picks me up. It's pretty funny. She tries to get him back sometimes.

'Well, he's not grown yet, has he?' she says after twelve sessions.

'You've not noticed his voice has broken?'

'Well . . . that's hardly connected, is it? I can't imagine he'll grow as fast as you say. It really isn't your job to tell him he'll be tall when I'll be the one who has to be there when he isn't.'

'He's just grown quarter of an inch,' he says. That shuts her up. But not as much as what happens when we get home. As we walk through the door, there's silence. Usually, when Cress is home, there's music on in every room. Mum puts her bag in the kitchen, and goes upstairs. I put on the kettle, then I hear Mum shout,

'Cress!'

I go to the bottom of the stairs, the door to Cress's room is open and Mum is standing in the doorway. There's a lot of activity in the room and Mum is shouting. She looks round and tells me to go back into the kitchen. I can see a flash of someone's naked leg. After a couple of minutes the three of them come downstairs: Mum, Cress and a boy from school. He looks worried. The doorbell goes, and it's the boy's mother. She and Mum argue on the doorstep.

136

'Peter has never been like this before.'

'Yes, but it's always the boys, isn't it?' Mum insists.

'Not necessarily,' she says. 'We'll have a very good talking to him, I can promise you. But I think yours might be . . . well . . . anyway.'

Mum doesn't like that much. The boy leaves with his mother.

I start to get headaches for no reason, but these feel different. They aren't the same as the ones that you get if you watch all the *Rocky* films in a row. I wake up in the middle of the night, my arms and legs aching like I've run a marathon in my sleep. I feel lethargic all the time. I sleep for thirteen hours, given the chance. Some days I knock everything over that I try to touch. And I grow seven inches in eighteen months.

6′

12.

SIX FOOT

Those fucking idiots the Mottisheads are coming round for dinner. God knows why I've got to stay in. Mum insists and she'll regret it, I'd arranged to go out with this girl, Rebecca. It's a Friday night, her parents are away, all that kind of thing. I'm upstairs trying to find a shirt that doesn't smell. Everything smells and nothing fits me. I pull all my clothes out of the drawers and can't find anything. I put some jeans on and storm into the bathroom. As I do, Cress steps out of the shower. She's reaching for a towel. She's naked. Thousands of hours go by.

'Marlow!'

'Yes?'

'What are you doing?'

'Oh, shit. Need a shirt,' I say and run out.

The idiots arrive. Donald and Heather.

'Hi, hi, hello everyone,' Heather has that kind of squinting smile, 'Wow, Marlow you've shot up, haven't you?' I just grunt. 'And Cress,' she continues, 'look at you! You'll break some hearts when you're older.' Cress smiles and goes red. Then she looks at me.

The women go into the kitchen and talk about periods or whatever, and the men walk round the garden. I can tell Dad hates this stuff now he doesn't really have to do it so much any more. After recovering from life by mending cars he's now doing travel writing for a newspaper. He has a little photo of himself in the piece and we always read it. He's been all over the world on trips. He always comes back suntanned and smiling. I'm glad he's doing something like this. He's got a lot younger since I used to know him. I watch Donald walk around the garden, practising his golf swing with an imaginary club. What kind of cock does that? Dad looks at him a bit funny, too. Who gave dull men the right to be mad. Donald rolls back on his heels the whole time, as if that would make his boring local newspaper tales any more interesting. God, I bet Dad is glad to be out of all that.

We sit down to eat. Donald talks about the mileage his new car does. I want to kill myself. Someone phones and Cress gets it, there's a lot of giggling and then ten hours later she comes back to the table. Donald is in the middle of one of his god awful stories: 'Well, I said, "To be honest. I. Don't. Give. A . . ."' he looks around the room, '". . . shit."' He whispers 'shit' and then looks at me, puts his hand on mine, smiles. 'Sorry, Marlow,' he patronises me.

'Don't be a cunt,' I say.

My mum shrieks at me.

'What? He's being a cunt,' I say.

'Don't say "cunt",' Dad says.

'Doyle, don't say that,' Mum says.

'What did he say?' Cress asks, aggravatingly.

'Cunt,' I say.

'Marlow!' Mum shrieks.

'I said "Shit" not "Cunt,"' Donald says, bewildered by the outbreak of war.

'You see, he just said "Cunt" – it might have been in a different context but either way that vile word has now passed to the innocent little ears of our blonde angel here,' I say, looking at Cress. She gives me the V sign. And pokes her tongue out just to make sure.

'He did *not* say . . .' Heather wavers. 'My husband would never say that. He said . . . shit.'

'Mind your language!' I say.

'What's a cunnilingus?' Cress asks.

'Same kind of area,' I say.

'It's a type of caterpillar, darling,' Mum says.

'Is it?' Heather says. 'What kind of caterpillar is that? I've never heard of cunnilingus.'

I try to stop laughing. Dad laughs as well.

'Doyle, don't laugh,' Mum shouts.

'Why's Doyle laughing?' Cress asks.

'It's *Dad*, darling. I don't know why he's laughing.'

'It's an insect,' I say to Cress. Mum looks relieved. 'It was around at the time of Fellatio Nelson,' I say.

'Who's Fellatio Nelson?' Cress asks.

'He was a—'

'Shut up!' Mum screams.

'Was Fellatio Horatio's brother?' Cress asks.

'His little friend,' I say.

'Doyle!' Mum shouts, 'Stop laughing and tell him to shut up.'

'Doyle!' Cress mimics.

'Oh, I *know* cunnilingus,' Heather pipes up after a short silence. 'It's not a caterpillar, it's a type of cloud.'

143

'No, it's an activity,' I say.

'Does Fellatio Nelson do it?' Cress asks.

'Oh yes. He does it, otherwise there's no fellatio for Nelson.'

My father is bright red and shaking with laughter. I love watching him laugh. I'd do anything to make him like this. It's my favourite thing in the world. I don't even remember him doing it until a couple of years ago. He really lets himself go. He looks like he's going to have a heart attack. Later when the conversation has calmed down, he'll sit for a while and then suddenly start laughing again, uncontrollably. By ten o'clock he has to go and have a lie down. The *Oh la la*s go home. As she leaves, Heather turns to me.

'Well, Marlow, you *have* changed. It was nice talking to you. I learnt a lot tonight.'

'Nothing Don couldn't teach you, I'm sure,' I say. She looks confused.

'Well, night everyone,' she says.

'Night,' we say like a happy family. A happy family in commuter-belt land, in nowhere land. Mum looks really pissed off so I go into my room. Cress comes in after a few minutes.

'That was funny,' she says.

'I didn't know you were in the shower.'

'No, I mean what you were saying.'

'What was I saying?'

'About cunnilingus and fellatio. I do know what those mean, you know. We have dictionaries too.'

'Why were you asking those stupid questions then?'

She shrugs.

144

'It was to egg me on, wasn't it? And it made you look innocent.'

'And Donald gets on my tits,' she adds, flicks her hair and walks out of the room. Women are cleverer than men.

'Don't say tits,' I shout after her. She pokes her head back in.

'Shit, I've forgotten how old you are,' I say.

'I'm fourteen, brother.'

Sixth form starts. And it turns out that sixth form girls, when you're there, aren't women at all. They're just little girls with too much make-up and too much hair. I passed some GCSEs and I failed some others. I didn't have to retake any, so that was one thing. I go over to my osteopath's house one afternoon and he makes me lunch. I meet his girlfriend who's unbelievable – she's so gorgeous. There's something I notice about her. It's something she has which I've never seen before. It's weird – not like anything any of the girls my age have. Maybe it's the way she walks, or something, I don't know. You just can't stop looking at her, watching her move. I feel very small when I look at her. The osteopath tells me lots of stuff about being a man, but not cheesy stuff like having a medallion and a hairy chest. He says maybe I didn't have much guidance when I was young. I'm not sure about that. He tells his girlfriend that I grew nearly a foot in sixteen months. Which isn't exactly true, but she looks impressed so I don't say anything. Considering he doesn't play rugby he has a great girlfriend. Maybe it works differently when you leave school.

145

That Neil kid is such a dick. One day we put all his books in the bin and hold lit matches over them, saying we'll drop them in. It's so funny I nearly piss my pants. We go into lunch. I sit in lunch with the girls and talk shit and they laugh like hell. I don't see Marty any more. He's a total Kev with his stupid hair. I don't see Rebecca any more. She's a slut. There's this girl in my year, she's called Lou and she's really nice. This rugby guy, Henry, one of the ones who used to put butter in my hair is going out with her. He tells this other guy that he loves her and wants to marry her. We go into lunch.

'Henry, is it true that you love Lou?' I ask him.

'Fuck off, Marlow,' he says. He just tells me to fuck off, no names, no strange sentences which I don't understand. Just a straight 'fuck off.' You can act against that.

'Henry, I heard she thinks you're too fat to marry. She doesn't want a fat baby. Like in *The Fly* when she gives birth to a slug.'

Everyone laughs. Henry goes red.

'If you marry her you'll have less time in the men's showers. Are you really ready for that kind of compromise?' I say. People around me, people scared of Henry, wet their pants. I'm just about to start something else but Lou sits down on the same table.

'Hi Henry,' she says, coyly. Henry cringes.

'Do you two lovebirds want to be together because we can all leave right now if you want,' I say. Henry shrugs. They laugh. I carry on.

'So tonight's the night then, Lou. Henry tells me,' I say, rubbing my hands together.

146

'What d'you mean?' she asks, looking angry.

'Oops, my mistake. Sorry.' I get up and take my tray to the dumping bin. There's one hatch for food, a big tray thing for cutlery, and a pile of plates. Someone chucks their cutlery down the chute that's only supposed to be for food. Someone cheers. Someone else throws a glass down there. People clap. So I tip my tray up and pour my cutlery *and* my plates down the chute, everyone laughs, starts cheering. Someone says, 'What about the tray?' So I snap the tray in half over my knee and chuck it down after the rest of the stuff. Everyone thinks that's amazing. I'm tall.

That night, as it's getting dark, I'm walking about at around six. Lou is sitting on the wall where everyone meets. I go up to her.

'Lou, I'm sorry about being stupid today,' I say, really putting it on.

'That's okay Marlow.' *Marlow* – another girl who knows my name. 'I finished with him today. I hate him,' she says.

'You want to go for a ciggy?' I ask her. She nods. It's in the bag. We walk to the football pitch, down one end where there are loads of trees. After two ciggies I kiss her and she tells me it's too soon. So I say loads of stuff I've heard on films and imagine how Henry is going to feel when he hears about this. I go for it and she doesn't mind. She gives me a hand job! That cheers her up; she's had a busy day. I walk back into the school grounds. Standing around by that wall is Parry. He looks wrong without his camouflage gear on. He left school a while back. He looks over at me. I look at him.

'All right,' he says. I nod.

'You?' I ask.

'Do I know you?' he asks.

'My balls are well acquainted with your boots. But I'm sure your violent outbursts helped you get over the dismay of having such a small penis.'

Old Parry wasn't ready for that. A few people gather around. He looks a bit lost. He looks like when you're with a girl and she's naked and you're doing stuff but you suddenly stop and she looks at you, and you can tell a thousand questions are going on in her mind, and she feels really exposed and really naked all of a sudden.

'What are you doing here? You don't even *go* to this school anymore?' I say.

He's speechless.

'I suppose you can come back and relive the glory days now you've had your arse kicked in the real world.' There's a really long pause. If bets were being taken then I'm winning, but there are still a few fence-sitters.

'At least I'm not a squeaky little virgin.'

'Do I sound squeaky?'

'Well, no.'

He walks over to me. The tension is wicked. Everyone is looking. He walks close. I look DOWN at him. I suddenly notice I have a chest, not like tits or anything, but it curves out in a convex before my stomach. I'm taller than him. Like in *Star Trek* when they teleport, I'm coming back, re-materialising for the first time since I was nine. You can see me, now. I am here.

'But you're still a fuckin' virgin,' he says. The tide turns against me a little bit. I need to pull something out now. Lou walks up behind me, puts her arms around me from behind and kisses my neck. She looks at Parry.

'Come back to marry Lieutenant what's-his-face finally?' she says. It kills them. The whole place applauds. The girl's got timing. Parry is dead. It's been a wonderful show. Thank you for watching. Please tip your waitress.

13.

BACK AT LARRY'S

The Larry Mullen guy is having another birthday. He's eighteen this year. It'll be my first party where I can stay out all night. I told my parents it was going to be a small thing and he had a spare room that I could stay in. They seemed to think that was okay, as long as I was around for when the Mottisheads came over for dinner. I'd already seen them once this year: how much punishment do I have to go through. I think Mrs Mottishead was rather taken with me. I'm quite a charmer.

Lou has started hanging around with me the whole time. And some of her girlfriends start talking to me when I walk past them. Joel looks over at me when they say, 'Hi, Marlow,' with a look in his eyes which I don't recognise.

'All of a sudden it's "Hi Marlow!"' Joel says. 'What's happening? And Lou is *total* rugby-boy's girl. What're you doing with her? The Berlin Wall is coming down.'

'I don't give a shit about the wall,' I say to him.

'You would've given a shit before—'

I wave him away, looking over at some girl who's walking towards us. I stare at her, waiting for her to say hello to me. Then she starts looking at me with an expression which seems to say, *why're you staring at me?*

'Hi Joel,' she says as she walks past us.

'See, you're not the king yet,' Joel says. 'Just because you've had a blowjob doesn't make you king.'

'You're not king, either,' I say.

'I don't want to be. I never wanted to be. This stuff shouldn't matter. If you want to get your end away then do it, but don't become a twat.' I've tuned out by now. I can't hear what boring crap he's going on about. He's talking like my osteopath. Then again, those two do get the lushest girlfriends. Joel was right about the blowjob though. Lou did it the other night. I take back what I was saying a couple of years ago about women in magazines being better. This was unbelievable. It was like I could feel every part of my body times a hundred. And it just didn't stop. I felt like I'd just joined some club. Some club Joel had founded when I was still five foot. When she made me come, a thousand things went through my mind. I wasn't in control, and I forgot to be embarrassed. I think back on it, when I'm walking along a street on a busy Saturday, into shops selling blank tapes and earbuds and washing machines; I watch cars go by and I watch people walk by, and all I can think of is how amazed I am, how amazed I am that there isn't complete chaos the entire time. How come there aren't orgies all day long? How come there are so many different magazine titles about boats and golf and climbing up mountains and anything you can think of – when there is *sex*. I keep waiting for everyone going about their daily business in shops, businesses, in the streets, to just stop dead and say a collective, 'Fuck it! Who are we kidding?' and start having sex there and then. And not

152

stop until it was time to eat. And then start again. What has been invented in order to stop this chaos happening in the supermarket every day? Well, have you seen some of the Swamp Things that hang around supermarkets? Still, what is it that has been created to be such a strong antidote? I never get the answer.

But there are a lot of things which I don't understand. I don't understand why Joel is all weird just because I'm going out with Lou and I occasionally say funny things about people in my year. I mean, everyone laughs, so what's the problem? Some of the girls are now worrying about what they'll all do when they leave school. I don't know what the hell I'm supposed to do. I can't understand how anyone makes any money in the world. We're supposed to be thinking about jobs already. There are companies that do the most tiny, minuscule things – I mean, someone is paid to evaluate the people who make glue which you put in between tiles. I don't understand how anyone makes any money at all. Sainsbury's and hookers – apart from those two, I haven't got a clue how anyone finds an idea they can sell to earn a living. I've not got any ideas like that so I suppose I'll starve.

The party. Simon's party. He still has Larry on his wall. Some things never change. Lou has flu so I'm there alone. I chat with a few people, I see Marty in the distance and he waves but doesn't come over to talk. Richie comes up to me but seems nervous around people from my school. I drink quite a lot of cider and throw up as usual. Then I feel better but really tired. As I know where the bedroom is I go up there and, no one around, I lie on the bed and doze off.

153

'Marlow,' a voice wakes me. I've got a headache.

'Marlow,' the voice says. I open one eye. There's a blur across the room, looking at me. A female blur.

'Who is it?'

'Are you blind?'

I sit up and try to focus. There's a young woman standing in the doorway. I can feel the dead apples from the cider, rotting in my mouth. I stand up, wobble a bit. It's not Lou.

'Peri?'

'Yup.'

'What are you doing here?'

'What are you doing being so bloody tall?'

'I grew,' I smile.

'No shit,' she says.

'Where've you, why've you, did you . . .' I say.

'Is that a U2 poster?'

'Yeah,' I say.

'I just phoned your house. Your sister said you were here,' she says. Peri sits on a chair by the desk in the corner of the room and lights a cigarette, nervously brushing the hair from her eyes.

'Peri, you look beautiful.'

'Shut up,' she says.

'Are you nervous about something?' I ask.

'No, I'm always like this,' she said. 'Are you nervous?'

'I can't believe you're here.'

'Your sister . . . she sounded so grown up on the phone.'

'She is.'

Peri is quiet again.

154

'Don't stop talking,' I say.

'I'm just going to tell you this, Marlow,' she says.

'Tell me what? Why you went away to another school?'

'Well, yes, that. And other things. I'd like to tell you. You're enough of a stranger now for me to talk to. I can't see the point in us talking about music or the weather when you'll be wondering the whole time what's going on.' She sounds so grown-up.

'God you look so different, Peri. You seem so different now, to when we were young.' She has on a low-cut top and I can see where her breasts push out the tight material. She looks like a young woman. Age gets to everyone, even me. A necklace hangs around her neck, she has some rings on her fingers.

'We're not that old,' she says.

'Do you remember what it was like when you were eight, or ten, or thirteen?' she asks.

'Not really.'

'You do, that's the thing. You do, but you block it out,' she takes a drag on her cigarette.

'So?'

'I can remember what it was like when I was really young.'

'Why are you telling me this?'

'What can you remember?'

'I don't know. Peri, what's going on? Shit, I've got a headache.'

'Do you want to talk about headaches or do you want to hear what I've got to say?'

155

'Well, I don't know what it is that you're saying, so it's difficult. Why don't you just say it?'

'You're a cocky shit, aren't you?' she says. I shut up. 'I remember being three,' she says.

'Well, good for you.'

'I remember exact events when I was six or seven,' she says. I give up and decide to play along.

'What do you remember?' I ask, sighing.

'Just things. Holidays. My mother throwing out some mouldy bread off a plate for the seagulls and letting go of the plate, the sound of it smashing on the ground. The sound of my parents laughing. The only time I remember them laughing.'

'And you were three or something?'

'Yes.'

She puts the lighter she's been fiddling with back together. She strikes it so a flame leaps out. She holds the gas button down as the little flame waves in the air. She comes over and lies on the bed, next to me. She stiffens when I try to put my arm around her, so I don't. It's hard to reconcile this with that warm mouth that kissed me, that never leaves my mind. I lie there for a while and then she seems to relax, but she's fallen asleep. Now she's perfectly quiet, her body shaking gently in the crisp, hard air in the room. I put my arm around her.

'What are you doing?' she wakes up.

'Putting my arm around you.'

'Why?'

'To keep you warm.'

'Oh.'

'So. Shall I?'

'Um. Can I think about it?'

'Yes.'

About ten minutes passes. She says, 'Can you put your arm around me?'

'Okay.'

I do and she feels stiff and tense. When I wake up she's sitting on the end of the bed, looking out through the window. It's still the middle of the night. She lies back down next to me.

'I've really missed you, Peri,' I say. 'I can't believe you just disappeared like that.' I'm still drunk. The words come out simply, but they aren't what I want to say. We lie on the bed and soon we're both dozing in and out of consciousness. A few hours later, first light is diffused by the condensation on the window. I wake up, the alcohol stinging my head. When Peri wakes up she says, 'You had your arm around me all night.'

'Did I?' I say.

'Yes.'

'So?'

'I'm just saying.' She looks out the window. 'I think I'm going to smoke more,' she says, like she's making her resolutions.

I sit up. 'I feel disgusting.'

'Me too.'

'I hate sleeping in my clothes.'

'Oh,' she sounds surprised, like she was talking about something else. 'Yeah, me too,' she says, vaguely.

'Do you want to smoke?'

'Have you got any?' she asks.

'No.'

'I've got some. Do you want one?'

'I'm still learning.' I focus my bleary eyes on her. 'You don't smile much,' I say. 'You used to be chirpy.'

'I was never chirpy,' she says.

We sit in silence for a second. There are a million things I want to say to her; ask her if she remembers that kiss we had years ago; why she never phoned me; why she was crying that day I went round to her house. Why some special doctor was coming to see her.

'I want to talk about our past,' she says.

'The kissing disease. Remember that?' I ask, excitedly.

'Of course I do,' she says, a small smile breaking. 'Of course I do. But we can talk about that later.'

'Well, okay,' I say.

'I was talking about what I could remember, from my past.'

'Yes,' I say.

'I can remember learning what lying was.'

'Eh?'

'I learnt to lie to people before you learnt to pee by yourself, probably.'

'Who did you lie to at that age?'

'I lied to everyone. I lied to my parents, my *uncles*. I had more uncles than anyone in the world. Oh, and *friends* of uncles.'

'What do you mean?'

'They weren't uncles, they were crappy doctors and therapists, but they were always introduced to me as uncles. I've lied to everyone: every therapist, doctor, parent and fake uncle.'

158

'I don't understand.'

'I can recall these things,' she says. She looks close to tears. The blue morning light is breaking through the window, which is fogged up. It comes through in streaks, where Peri has drawn a smiley face with her finger in the condensation. The face looks alive with the morning light coming through it. As the room warms up, it melts the condensation lines which Peri's finger has traced. The lines start to bleed. Giant tears disfigure the face as they fall from the eyes. The small electric heater fan we put on when we woke up is whirring away in the corner. It's still so cold, and the fan picks up the cigarette smoke and blows it around the room.

'I can remember the colours of the walls, the sound of the alarm. I can remember their faces, everything,' she says.

'Peri, I don't know what you're talking about.'

We sit in the thick morning mist of smoke, heat and damp slept-in clothes. She looks at me.

'I remember them shaving my head.'

There's a pause. 'What do you mean, shaving your hair?'

She just looks at me.

'Oh my God. You're that girl aren't you?'

'Yes.'

'Oh my God,' I say. 'Oh my God,' I say again.

14.

AIR JORDANS

Before this growing spurt – which at the moment looks like I'm going to be ten foot tall – Cress was catching up with me fast. Somehow, for a little while, she became older than me. I don't know how this happened. Cress was tall, like Dad, and had developed. I don't want to use the word tits because she's my sister and everything, but Cress had breasts which I just imagined she would never have. I mean, the women in magazines had them. It turned out girls in real life had them – I'd seen that with my *own* eyes. Mothers had big practical ones. But my sister, surely she shouldn't have them. But she did, and her hair was long now with no stupid perm any more and she was tall; she'd lost all that pudginess – which Mum said was unusually early. I thought she looked like she didn't quite fit herself, if you know what I mean. But people must have thought she looked nice or something as she was always getting asked out, and one day in Boots some guy asked her if she was a model and Mum hit him with her basket as she thought he was one of those perverts you hear about. He was from some agency, in the end. But it was strange. For a while Sausage had overtaken me – she seemed to be nearly a woman. I was a boy, still waiting for my instructions on how to be a man. It took me twelve months to catch up with her. Then I left her far behind. But I could remember walking along the street when I was a child, looking at Sausage's sticky little hand in mine. And I'd look down at her and she'd screw her face up if I was walking too quickly or squeezing her hand too tightly. And she was always dressed up in stupid, unsuitable clothes. Then, not so long ago, before the osteopath worked his magic, I'd walk down the street with her. I'd be with Cress who was taller than me, and unlike all her friends she hardly wore any make-up. She'd have on simple clothes. Her hair was cut onto her shoulders and she wore blue a lot. And as we walked along men would look at her. Not teenagers, not people my age or older. Men. I'd see them look at her legs, her face, her arms, her chest and it would me feel sick. I couldn't stand the thought of them looking at Sausage that way. And she'd react, or rather not react at all, like she was used to it. Not in a snobbish way – she wouldn't really take much notice of them. If someone made a comment or someone came up to her she'd look embarrassed but be kind to them. Or she'd wave. And I'd want to push them away from her but they were men. They were men the same size as Dad and they probably had to shave twice a day, and could probably fill out forms like it was really easy and they were all gawking at Cress.

It still feels weird walking with her. But at last I'm taller than her. Although I realise it wasn't because I was smaller that I was less noticeable than her – I'll always be less noticeable.

I open my eyes. I can hear Cress's voice talking to

162

Mum. I got home at eight this morning, and went to bed straight away. Now I'm lying here, my eyes wide, my mind racing. I'm still in my clothes. I don't know how to react; I don't know what to do. It feels like I'm waiting for something to kick in. I sit up in bed, put my head in my hands. I can still taste the cider. I take off my clothes. They're damp with drink and sweat and the night. They're damp with stories and confessions and shock. I walk out of my room, and into the bathroom. In the shower I piece together little moments from the night, but the alcohol keeps kicking in and interrupting. I'm not sure if I want to cry or not, or if it's just going to happen. I stand in the shower and look down at all the bloody hair which I still can't get used to. I mean, I had it where you need it for ages. I had that when I was short. But it's spread now, up to my belly button. And right in the middle of my chest. I let the water splash down on my back and put shampoo in my hair.

When I get downstairs Mum asks me if I had a good time at Simon's party. It's Sunday morning and Cress is now out at her dancing class. Dad is away. Church has been abandoned. He's left a book by the telephone, with a note. It says: 'Marlow, sorry I didn't say goodbye. Hope you have a good party, and make sure you read this before I get back – there's some things we need to talk about.' The book is by Noam Chomsky. Dad has given me stuff like that to read before. I think it was so he had some more ammunition against the Mottishead dinner parties. Now, I get the feeling he thinks I've done something wrong.

'So I expect Lou was there,' Mum says, smiling.

'Actually she wasn't.'

'Oh, who did you see? Anyone?'

'Just Peri,' I say, casually.

'No, really?'

'Really.'

'You're joking?'

I can't think of any way to say it, so I just say it.

'Do you remember, years ago, when we went to get my lizard in that arcade, that knackered old place that's derelict.

'I remember the lizards,' she says, chirpily.

'You don't remember when we were shopping with Cress and the alarms all went off?'

'Well, maybe . . .'

'You *do* remember. You're not going to believe this, *you will* not believe this. I was talking to Peri last night.'

'What d'you want for lunch?' Mum asks.

'Are you listening to me?' I say.

'Look, Marlow. I know what you're going to say. I know about it. Her mother told me.'

I sit there, looking blank.

'What do you know about?'

'I know what you're going to say. Peri's mother told me.'

'And you didn't tell me?'

'Not at that age, no. You were so young.'

'Why didn't you tell me now? That's why Peri kept going to different schools, why she was so unhappy.'

'Well, I didn't think you'd even remember that day.'

'I can't believe this,' I say. 'Did Peri know you knew?'

'I don't think so. Her mother thought she didn't remember. That's what she hoped.'

'Well, guess what?' I say, sarcastically. 'She does.'

Mum avoids my eyes.

'So when she was being carted around to different schools, and she was disruptive and unhappy, they didn't think that there was something lingering there?'

'Marlow, I'm not a bloody psychiatrist. I just don't know.'

'Well, this is a can of worms.'

The front door bangs. Cress walks in to the room. 'Worms?' she says.

'Nothing, darling,' Mum says. 'I don't want to talk about this any more,' she turns to me.

'Don't *nothing* me,' Cress says. 'What are you talking about?'

'Mum thinks Dad has worms from when he was in Pakistan,' I say.

'Doyle has worms?'

'*Dad*. And no he doesn't.' I catch a glimpse of my mother's thankful face, looking at me. I didn't owe her that. I haven't seen that face many times. I don't remember ever talking to Cress about that day. I don't think she ever asked.

'You want to go to the shops this afternoon?' Cress asks. I look over at Mum, who looks like she wants to talk more.

'Let's go,' I say. Cress and me walk out the door.

'You all right?' she says, as we walk down the street. 'You look, you don't look normal.'

'I'm fine.'

'Talk to me.'

'It's nothing,' I say. We get on the bus, and sit together. I can't bring myself to say anything at all. When we get to the main street, Cress wanders off into some shops by herself. I go into a shoe shop. There's a group of thirteen-year-olds wearing tracksuits, walking around the shop, looking dodgy. The assistant comes up to me, pushy.

'What are you looking for?'

'Um, some trainers.'

'What kind?'

'I don't know. Am I allowed to have a look around?'

He backs off and I patrol the racks of rubber. I suddenly have the desire to own a pair of Nikes. I've been told they exploit workers in East Asia; I know they incorporate youth rebellion and culture from black New Yorkers and then sell it back to them at inflated prices. I know all of this. But suddenly I want those air soles, that swoosh – which is practically the symbol of the devil, according to Joel – and I want the bounce and the extra height. I want, I want, I want.

So I buy them.

'In the box, or d'you want to wear them?' the assistant says.

'I'll wear them,' I say. As I put my old shoes back in the box I get an horrific rush of fear. I start shaking. I can see Peri as she is now, but with her hair shaved. I can smell the arcade. All of my body is jittering. In my mind the image of Peri fades into Cress and back into Peri again. Peri's angled cheekbones morph into Cress's more rounded face, her wide mouth. But the green eyes stay the same. I look over to the door of the shop. The security guard is manhandling one of the young kids back into the shop. Eventually, someone switches the shop alarm off. The guard unpacks the kid's bag and a pair of trainers fall out.

I pay for my Air Jordans. They cost six million quid. I painted the whole of the Mottisheads' house over a weekend for these babies. A different assistant comes up to me. He's wearing baggy tracksuit bottoms and a baseball cap.

He says, 'You play?'

'Yeah,' I say. 'Haven't played for a while.'

'You a centre?'

'Shit, no. I'm not tall enough?'

'What are you . . . six two?'

'Not sure, haven't measured recently.'

He beckons for me to follow him. There is a tape measure stuck to a wall at the far end of the shop, right by the long thin mirror. I stand with my back to it and he makes a pencil mark against the wall. I walk away from it.

'Well, with those shoes on you are . . . six foot, two and one eighth inches.' I stand there, pretty amazed.

'If you want to play, come and play with us. We close in five minutes. Wait around.'

I go off to find Cress, who's chatting to a friend she must have bumped into in Warehouse. I interrupt them, tell them I'm going to play basketball. Cress raises an eyebrow. I find out later that she wasn't talking to a friend; she'd just met a girl and they'd started talking – unbelievable.

There's ten or twelve of us down at the playground.

There's a black kid with straight, shiny hair. I can't take my eyes off him. I watch them all play around, basketballs flying in different directions. The kid comes over to me.

'Marlow,' he says.

'Fuck, Reggie?'

'How's it goin'?'

'Pretty good,' I say. 'Haven't seen you for years. You been all right?'

'Yeah,' he smiles. 'It's so cool seeing you. Come and play.' I follow him. Two teams of five start battling. I was last pick, but it wasn't like at school where you stand there, all alone in the whistling wind, while perfect prefect boys who'll have sad and fat lives are picked before you. It was all relaxed. We get going. It's been so long since I've played. Every time I get the ball, I try to set up a play for someone else. They make jokes about my shoes, how new they are, but they're all smiling and messing around and I make a couple of steals and suddenly I'm marked constantly and it gets physical. I'm standing, dribbling the ball, and this guy knocks into me as he guards me and I don't budge. My legs stay rooted into the ground like a tree. Like Colonel Wintle. On one of the steals I feed the ball to Reggie who gracefully lays it up and in, his black hair flowing behind him, just like when we'd run around the playground as children. The other time I run down the court but pull up short – I'm too scared to try and dunk it – and I throw it, not beautifully, but efficiently, and it goes in. A little cheer goes up from Reggie as we pursue the ball down the court.

168

'I knew you'd be a tall bastard,' Reggie says. 'You were always the biggest in primary school.'

'Well actually I—'

'I can't imagine what's it's like being short, can you?' he says.

15.

WELCOME TO PARADISE

Peri drives a brown Austin Maxi. That's a tough old piece of shit.

'Whose is this?' I ask.

'It's mine,' she says. 'A guilt present.'

'They don't feel too guilty, then, do they?'

'I don't see your car.'

'What colour is this? British Racing sludge?'

Peri looks over at me. Her face is angled, sharp. Her blonde-brown hair is pulled back into a ponytail. She's squinting, looking out onto the dark road.

'Where are we going, Peri?'

'On a Famous Five adventure.'

'When did you pass your test?'

'Year ago.'

'Really? Where are we going, Peri?'

She keeps driving, her eyes lit by reflections of car lights in the rear-view mirror. She pulls into a deserted car park, potholed, with weeds growing up through the tarmac.

Dust particles form little dry islands on my lips. The floor is hard and unforgiving. Smooth concrete stretches out forever. My knees ache, the cartilage and skin being ground away by the hard floor. Dust is in my eyes.

Around me graffiti covers walls which have discoloured from white to yellow, and have finally given up on brown and started to crumble away. Peri's skin tastes of lemon. My lips, despite the dry dust, make wet patches on her neck. When her tongue is in my mouth it feels as hot as it was when it was infected with the kissing disease. My fingers go into her knickers and find a soft mound of hair, then I slide them up and down the slit between her legs. My mouth is over hers the whole time. We're the weirdest people I have ever met.

'C'mon,' Peri says. I pull her knickers down to her knees. She kicks them off. I grab a handful of my boxer shorts and pull them down. I roll back on top of her. I look at her for a moment. I move closer and closer, our stomachs touching. She just whispers, 'Can you imagine,' as I slide into her. I feel like I'm protected. I gasp. She doesn't notice. I slide all the way into her. Stop. My knees almost give way, I'm sure my eyes cross. I forget to even start moving again – I'm happy to just lie there, deep inside her. She starts wiggling her hips and it sends mad sparks across my body. I can feel my ears and my eyes, my hair follicles and my fingernails and everything that I don't remember ever feeling anything in before. I look into her infinite green eyes and they look like my whole body feels: cool and hot, alien and familiar. No friction and frantic abrasion. I start moving and she joins in, wiggling under me, in time to my rhythms. I can feel myself tense, almost unable to move, and she coaxes me on, which I do until I come. I keep moving inside her, feeling the orgasm lasting for a year or a millisecond. I just came inside her.

We walk around for a while afterwards.

'Peri, this is the weirdest thing.'

'I thought it'd shake you out of your arrogance.'

'What would?'

'What we just did. This place. Everything.'

I kick a piece of old tile across the floor. It shoots away like a hockey puck. It reminds me of my old watch, being thrown on the floor, being kicked, and skidding along the smooth surface. All around us there's smashed glass, fragments of a venture which never quite made it. I hold her hand and memories come back as we walk up and down old, broken escalators. The Paradise Arcade doesn't look like it's been used for ten years. I can hear a clanking sound as we walk up the static metal steps. I wonder if it's the ghost of a slinky, haunting the escalator forever.

'Let's go this way,' Peri says. I follow her. Half a sign hangs on the wall.

'What's in there?'

'The mens' toilets.'

'Are you joking?'

'Let's go in there.'

'I think that's called a bit too much confronting your demons.'

'My demons aren't in there any more. They're finally in prison,' she says. We get as far as the entrance and her hand holds mine so tightly I can feel my knuckles click under the pressure. She stops moving. I look over at her as silent sobs, muted tears come from her eyes. I feel like I'm still inside her. Only her. She doesn't move her face; she looks straight ahead.

'Do you want me to go in?' I say.

'I don't know what I want.'

'Why did we come here in the first place?' I ask.

'I'm not sure. I don't always have a reason for everything I do. I liked the way you broke that window to get in here though,' she says. 'Boys throw bricks well.'

'Pleasure. Isn't this just more upsetting? And slightly psychotic?'

'I'm fine.'

'Did you ever come back here since it happened?'

'Only once, years later,' she says walking slowly in circles around me, like she's balancing on a tightrope. 'I didn't get past the front door. That was when it was still open and working. I kept thinking about what happened to the other girl. That haunted me.'

'The other girl?'

'I used to hope they'd uncover who she was, so I could go and talk to her,' she says.

'I didn't even know anyone else was taken. Did it ever come out?'

'Don't you remember the newspapers?'

'I didn't read a lot of papers at that age.'

'No, I mean later.'

'No. What were you doing? Going to the library and looking it up on the microfiche?'

'Yes.'

'Bloody hell. So what happened with the other girl?'

'They took her. It was a few months before me. I think they assaulted her – but some shopper, some guy, saw them and went after them. And they ran, leaving the girl.'

My hands are in my pockets, I'm looking at the ground. 'Well, let's go Peri. C'mon.'

'One second,' she says, smiling. She lets go of my hand, walks through the little entrance into the toilets. I can see her reflected back to me in the large mirrors by the washbasins. Parts of them are still reflective, other bits just covered in moss and algae. The whole place looks like the bottom of an old fish tank when you empty the water out. Organisms are busy eating away at the structure, at all the things that happened here. Eventually the whole building, and all its memories and events and ghosts, will be eaten alive by microscopic organisms, as the chain continues, and another arcade is built.

Her hair hangs down her back, ravaged by the dust and dirt of the floor, tangled with the sweat from my hands. The rugged, tough beauty of her face, the seen-it-all look in her young eyes is reflected in the old mirror. Her face – an older face, fading in and out of a young complexion – shows no emotion for the seconds before she turns right to where the cubicles are, and then goes out of sight. I stand there and don't move. I don't move for a few moments, and I only do move when I hear her scream.

16.

A FRIEND OF BEAUTIES

At school it was becoming more and more difficult to fit into the wardrobe. I realised, later, that I was caught so many times, got punished so many times, that I couldn't exactly remember why I tried to miss chapel and hide in a cramped box in the first place. Joel got expelled. His uncle used to drop him off at school, and Joel would smoke a fag on the way in the car. They said that he couldn't do that, and why was he still wearing a *Nazi Punks Fuck Off* T-shirt visible under his school shirt, when he had been told not to. So the next day, after his uncle had dropped him off, he took his school shirt off, revealing his *Too Drunk to Fuck* T-shirt, sparked up a spliff and walked into chapel. We were singing *Jerusalem*. I was glad I wasn't in the wardrobe that day. Joel lasted about forty-five seconds before he was carted off and expelled. That was the end of him.

With Joel gone I get a bit of work done, although in a way my education stops. The problem with my A levels is that I chose subjects which meant I wouldn't be around people who didn't like me – everyone. So I end up doing two useless subjects, but I do English because none of those bastards wanted to do that. It is the same way that I chose my GCSE specialisations – whatever they were doing, I did something else.

My English teacher is great. He's a scary man, although he isn't to look at. He isn't so much a teacher of English, as a sergeant of literature. He makes you feel that if you don't do the required reading there is some punishment, above what he could dish out, above what the school could dish out, probably above what God could dish out. There is some punishment which the ghosts of D. H. Lawrence, William Shakespeare and T. S. Eliot have devised. A kind of divine judgement, a day of reckoning for which Malcolm Gabbert MA is the prophet. He makes you feel like you are personally insulting these dead giants of literature by not doing the work. It works – I've no idea how. We do the work.

There was me in the class, and fifteen girls. Girls must like English. They were really good at it, too. The first day I walked in, I saw a sea of long hair and badly applied make-up and I nearly choked. But they seemed friendly enough. Lou had given me good reviews so I found myself sitting next to the girls and, instead of trying to chat them up, I'd say stupid things which they laughed at. Maybe they thought I was funny. Maybe they were just being nice. Sometimes girls are just being nice.

You had to be on guard in these lessons.

'What's the point he's making at the end of *The Rainbow?*'

Someone has a go: 'By the end of the book—'

'Novel!' Gabbert MA shouts. The volunteer is now shaking, and like in that game when you can't say yes or no, she knows she can't avoid that word. But she has to carry on.

'By the end of the *novel* you realise that he's been saying, throughout the book, oh . . .'

'Novel! Delia Smith writes books. D. H. Lawrence writes novels!'

When we finally find out what point he was making at the end of the novel we start something new.

'Someone define satire,' Gabbert MA says. The girl sitting next to me whispers, 'What is it?'

'Sarcasm,' I whisper back. She attracts the teacher's attention.

'Sarcasm,' she says.

'NO!' screams Gabbert MA and indeed the wrath of Alexander Pope falls upon that young maiden. She punches me in the arm, 'Idiot!' she smiles. I tell her that's what I thought it was.

It was the start of six weeks of Alexander Pope boot camp. It seemed to me that he was a genius, no doubt. I mean, he hated the society he lived in, but he was drawn to it. And on the inside cover he, or someone, described himself as, 'A man of letters and a friend of beauties.' Now, I don't exactly know how that translates nowadays, but it sounded like a pretty good thing to be, if you couldn't be Prince. A man of letters and a friend of beauties. It turned out that I had a gift for iambic pentameters. I could just do them, hear them, and notice if something was one beat too long or short. When we did our imitations of Pope the girls all gave me their lines for me to check over for the timings. That way I learned their names and they seemed really grateful. I could just hear those beats so easily – I couldn't understand why they found it hard. I got a couple of snogs out of all this: taking an exercise book back to a girl who had forgotten it, going for a ciggie on the football pitch, that sort of thing.

They were pretty girls, too. They wrote nice lines, much better than me, but they couldn't do the timings. One of them said my rhythm was famous and they all laughed. It seemed to be important to them. Anyway, writing iambics and nice girls – I thought Alexander would approve. Gabbert set us so much work that we didn't have any time for the other subjects. We complained and his answer was, 'This is Literature!' which seemed to sort it out. Our other subjects would have to suffer. And so I spent hours with that class, with those strange young women who, I realised, ran the school with the trick of making it seem they weren't even involved. I studied them; I watched the way they moved and I became good friends with them. And because I was friends with them, I was friends with everyone. I spent less time with other people and probably seemed more aloof than I was.

'You're an arrogant git!' Joel said, sitting in chapel a couple of days before he was expelled.

'Why am I arrogant?'

'You walk round like you own the place. I saw you the other day, ripping the shit into someone, making them feel so small. I watched their face look down at the ground, their eyes sink in. They looked like a bloody tortoise when it goes into its shell.'

'That was just whatshisname, he's a dick.

'You don't get it, do you?'

*   *   *

I'm sitting at home, eating dinner. The whole family is
there. Cress is in a new phase. She's gone all nice and
kind. Dad is back and looking really brown. When
we've finished eating Dad stays at the table, drinking
his coffee, smoking his cigarette. No one looks better
with a cigarette than he does.

'Marlow . . .'

'This doesn't sound promising.'

'We've noticed a real change in you,' he says.

'Okay.'

'I'm a little concerned. You seem happier. Are you
happier?'

'You're concerned about me being happy?'

'No. I'm glad that you are. I think you've come
out the other side with no help. But sometimes you
can come out too far the other side. Know what I
mean?'

'No.'

'You know, children are basically Nazis.'

'What?'

'They're basically Nazis until they're told otherwise.
At primary school they hit each other, are selfish, tease,
torment, hurt and break anyone or anything that's
weaker or different than them, or that doesn't do what
they want.'

'I suppose that's true.'

'It is. And it's the parents' job to make sure that
they learn values and treat people who are different
from them with respect. Isn't that what your music
preaches? And you were friends with Reggie, before
you even realised he was black.'

'I'm not a racist.'

'I think, without guidance, children show all the signs of what, later, causes prejudice, hate, bigotry and war.'

'Okay, Dad.'

He says this next bit really calmly. 'Then why are you treating your peers with no respect?'

'What d'you mean?'

'I hear that you've been making some kids' lives a real misery. You're nearly an adult.'

'They're sixteen, seventeen years old.'

'Makes no difference. Don't you remember being on the other end?'

'Sort of.'

'And didn't it feel like it would last forever?'

'Yeah.'

'So think about that. Because this stuff carries on in later life, too. There were people in my office, grown men like me, afraid of someone younger, someone smaller than them. It happens everywhere. I thought I'd taught you how to behave when you were younger. Don't shrug at me.'

'Sorry,' I look at my boots.

'I think Marlow is great,' a voice pipes up. I look round, see Cress. She knows about what happened to me at school. I never told her, but I'm sure she just knows. I think about whether I should bring up Peri. Dad, guess what? I had sex with Peri in the arcade. I decide to say nothing.

17.

I DREAM OF SADDAM

The Mottisheads are back. Within a few minutes, Don is going off on one about the Gulf War. He's written a piece about it for the paper, so now he's an expert. He hasn't been out there.

'It's so difficult, though,' Don starts, 'Even on television news our journalists are under Iraqi censorship.' He turns to me, and I brace myself to be patronised. 'You've probably heard the newsreaders, Marlow, say: "this report is subject to Iraqi censorship."'

I look at him like he's a bag of shit.

'I don't know why,' Dad says, finishing a mouthful, 'they don't say: "This report is also subject to British government censorship so if you want the truth you can sing for it".'

I love it when Dad saves me. That's what I wanted to say.

'Well, that's a little extreme. I mean, the Iraqis, the um . . . Saddam, you know they're under a regime and we're part of a democracy.'

'But freedom and democracy aren't the same thing,' I say. 'Those reporters aren't free.' Dad gives me a *that's my boy* look. Mum asks if anyone wants more parsnips.

'It's part of the demonising of the enemy, isn't it, Dad?'

I say. Cress's eyes go from me to Don to Dad like some weird tennis match.

'You can write what you like about the war, can you, Don?' Dad says.

'Well, I mean, no. Well . . .'

'It wasn't long ago that the Russians were shown in that way.'

'Now the Russians are a lovely people,' Don says. 'I went to Moscow and—'

'What, they're *all* lovely, are they?' Dad says. He laughs to himself. How much more punishment do the Mottisheads require. What is it going to take? Dad shagging Mrs Mottishead on the table before they finally fuck off and stop bothering us. I don't know why Mum keeps bloody inviting them.

'How bombing Iraqi villagers helps get rid of a dictator I'll never know,' Dad says.

'It'll work,' Don says. 'It just takes time.'

'They'll get him out of Kuwait. But he'll still be around, unfortunately. And I guarantee you it will ensure another few years of his power. His popularity will go up.'

'Let's change the subject,' Mum says. There's silence for a few moments. Then Cress speaks. She's been quiet all evening. She says:

'So, there's a fair chance that we'll all have a lifetime of eternal nothingness after we die. That's gonna be a fucker, isn't it?' she says, sweetly somehow.

Dad spits his food out and nearly chokes to death.

'Who said that!' Mum shouts.

'I heard Marlow say it the other day,' Cress says quickly, putting her innocent eyes on full. The cow stole my line. She takes a triumphant sip of wine, which Mum snatches away from her. She's been drinking secretly all evening, and while Dad is still laughing his head off Cress looks more and more ill. Dad stops laughing when she passes out. Half an hour later the rest of the table, me included, are still sitting in total silence, while the doctor tells Mum that Cress is allergic to alcohol. She's fine the next morning, but I don't think we'll ever see the Mottisheads again.

Exams approach. I can't concentrate for the period of time it takes to do the papers. I keep thinking about what I see on television every evening: the fallout from our new nice-bombs and kind-bombs litter the screen, litter our conscience for only a second. I start to feel angry as our dull, thin leader says that we have no quarrel with the people themselves. I watch them wander, lost – absolutely and totally lost – around the rubble made by our bombers. And, in the distance, fresh clusters of violent, explosive confetti are being dropped while the Iraqis' guns fire uselessly into the night. I watch Tony Benn talk on TV.

Peri's parents found out, eventually, that she had visited what was left of the arcade with me and they went insane. She managed not to tell them that we had sex in there – I don't think that's the sort of thing parents regard as healthy. She called me a couple of times, said that she was having treatment and was going to sit her A Levels at home, then go, probably to Scotland or somewhere, to university. Peri was clever; she probably didn't need to do very much work to get in as it was. She spent long periods in places in the country. People seem to think that trees will solve everything. These places' addresses weren't given to me or to anyone. Her mother spoke curtly with me on the phone and I gave up. It was never mentioned in our house again. If I tried to talk to Mum about it, she would just say it's all in the past.

Before the real exams, we do mock papers for weeks. Can you believe Saccy is still going? He taught my mate Adam A level chemistry. Adam used to get Fs in his chemistry papers. Thing was, only one other girl chose chemistry at that level, so they had mostly personal tutorials. Adam: a kind, laconic boy, would go in to see Saccy and shoot the breeze over a couple of coffee-stained mugs of neat vodka. Doesn't make your breath smell. After Adam's series of Fs in the practice papers, he decided there was only one thing for it. So, on the day of the exam, he drank half a bottle of vodka beforehand and got an E. He said he was very pleased. Saccy said it was great news, and true chemists are creative scientists and cannot be judged by these mediocre exams. Then he took Adam up the pub for the evening. On the day of the results, the papers were full of pictures of hundreds of Philippas all running about and crying, flicking their hair, holding their results. No pictures of boys, though. They were all still in bed like me.

I passed a couple of mine. I got my English, I got my rhythm.

A few days before the end of term, when most of the exams were wrapped up and people were hanging around, I'm sitting on the grass when I hear a familiar

'Oi, fuckhead.' I look around. It's Joel. He looks a lot older.

'How're you doing?' he says.

'I'm okay.'

'I hear you're not hanging around with those gits any more.'

'Where did you hear that?' I'm smiling.

'I'm fucking your head girl.'

'Really?'

Joel gives me a 'would I lie?' look.

'Rebecca says you don't go around ripping the shit out of everyone anymore.'

'I never did.'

'Yes, you did. And you were going out with those terrible girls.'

'You're going out with the head girl!'

'Yeah, but I take her to Fugazi concerts and then fuck her on the way home.'

'How romantic, Joel. You're a special guy.'

Joel smiles at me, 'Plus she's not going to Oxford like they want her to. She's coming to check out what's left of the Berlin Wall with me. So how's the exams going?'

'Shit. Adam is getting drunk beforehand. I think I might join him.'

'What I want to know is,' Joel says, 'why you changed and became quiet again just as you were becoming loud and annoying and noticed.'

'Oh, it's this girl.'

'Tell me about her.'

'No way.'

'Okay, let's go to the pub and you can tell me about her.'

'I'm not very good at drinking,' I say.

We sit in the pub, Joel looking cool with his drink, me looking awkward and waiting to get chucked out. Joel sips his beer.

'I hear your sister's grown up,' he smirks.

'Don't fuckin' think about it.'

'All right mate, calm down, I'm only fucking around. Jesus.' He takes another sip. 'So tell me about this girl.'

So I do. I tell him the whole story from beginning to end. It takes three pints each to get through it, and I'm talking really quickly. Joel leans forward the whole time, eating up every word, with a serious expression on his face. By the time I finish the story, the pub has filled up. I leave out the bit about her and me doing it in the arcade.

'That's the most unbelievable thing I've ever heard.'

'Well, there you go.'

'That the most unbelievable thing I've ever heard,' Joel says, this time stressing different words as he says it.

'So all that time Peri's parents didn't know that she remembered what happened.'

'Basically.'

'That's insane. Did she always know, or did she remember it as she got older?'

'Always knew.'

'What are her parents like?'

'Pretty strange. Quite rich, I think. Into drugs.'

'So where are you going now?' Joel says.

'I think, to Liverpool.'

'You think.'

'I don't know if I'll go when the day comes. I don't know if my grades are good enough.'

'You'll get in, they want people. So many people go now, and there are all these courses which are just money-earners for the colleges.'

'Thanks, cheerful.'

'No, I'm sure you'll have a good time.'

'And what are you going to do?'

'Well,' he says, taking a toke on his fag. 'I think I'm going to tour with this band I'm in, we've got some record company interest. Then, I don't know what after that.'

'Well, stay in touch, yeah? My parents will always have my number.' I shake Joel's hand as we leave. It's the first time I've shaken a friend's hand for real. And I mean it. I feel like a man. A bit. I get home and feel drunk. Upstairs, I scrawl pissed pictures of figures without faces. I look out the window as I scribble on the paper, I won't be sorry to get out of this town of roundabouts and not much else. There are roundabouts everywhere, to make you think you're doing something. But you're just going round and round in circles. When your washing machine isn't working or your computer has crashed, then the people who you're talking to on the phone are probably sitting in nondescript buildings in this town. I never noticed this before, but the best thing you can say about this place is that it has good car parking. I want to get away from the places around here and the stagnant history which seems to attach itself to its inhabitants like Velcro. I want to leave and I hope when I return a giant parasite has eaten the whole place, and we can put soulless commuter-belt towns down to a bad experiment and move on. Where there's no soul to a place, no heart, anything can happen. People give up.

Bit by bit the day gets nearer. The day when I leave home. And although I'd thought along the way that I might just not go to university, I couldn't really think of what else to do. So I went. On the actual day I leave home, Mum calls me into the kitchen. Cress is already moving things out of my room and putting hers in there. I thought if I let her, then she'd end up packing for me. And she did. Mum wants to say something, but I make an excuse and go upstairs to get my bags.

'Moved in then?' I say, laughing.

'Yup,' Cress says. I sit down on my bed. She sits down by me.

'You don't mind me in here, do you? You can have my room when you come back.'

'You're welcome to it.'

'Thanks, mate,' she says, and slaps my leg, leaves her hand there, on the inside of my thigh. She kisses me on the cheek, puts her arms around my neck. I can smell her hair, as it brushes against my face.

'You can take your hand off my leg now,' I say.

'Ooh,' she says, and moves her hand. 'Sorry,' she says, kind of faking embarrassment. I stand up. I'm suddenly relieved she took her hand away when she did. I pause for a second, my brain tries to process something but is blocked, like when you think about space going on forever and your mind almost switches off before the moment of comprehension. I can feel a headache coming on. I make for the door.

'Marlow,' she calls after me.

'What?' I snap.

'I'll miss you,' she says.

18.

PROTECTION

I found myself at university. It wasn't much more emotional than that. I don't remember expressing any particular feeling about college. I just found myself there. You can do degrees in anything. Grim was talking total shit. I decided to do mine in photography. I lasted a few months in Liverpool. I sat there on the first day, watching people get their meals in the canteen, and I thought: who are these people? All the faces, dyed-blue hair, dreadlocks, shaved heads, combat trousers, army jackets, polo shirts, side partings, brown brogues, Doc Martens – they all walked around, these people in my year. And I didn't see their faces, I saw the faces that I'd blanked out from years before. For the first time I saw the faces and heard the names of the aggressors in my head. The blurs which were ingrained in my memory became clearer, like the picture of Jesus that was on my bedroom wall, which Mum had cleaned up, and which now haunts some godson of hers.

It came to me, slowly.

In the café there was a guy wearing a sports blazer – and in him I saw Andrew Hosey. Andrew had a slight lisp, at least when he was young. His short dark hair and pale skin merged into one in a cluster of spots along the line of his forehead. It was that forehead I slapped back when I was in the classroom, specks of blood appearing on my hand from where I had broken his acne-riddled flesh. In an upright, uptight figure standing by the coffee machine I saw Parry and what his face looked like after I'd made him look stupid in front of his friends.

I remembered Tony York, who died in a car crash three days after his eighteenth birthday. He was the one who threw my pencil case around the room in the French lesson. He went through the windscreen on a Saturday morning. Michael Tillmore: he was the one who came into the bathroom while I was soaking my bloody eyebrow. He joined the army; finally his skill for beating up people who were different from him had found the perfect outlet. He stood on an unexploded shell while on exercise in North Wales and lost his foot. The rugby star, Henry Mason, the golden boy, was engaged to the head girl. That made the school magazine front page. I heard that Joel would still occasionally see that girl. So I don't hold out much hope for that marriage: one minute at a regatta, the next a punk gig. And over the years to come, I would see the lives and hopes of people who were giants crumble into accountancy, into mediocrity, into death and into boredom. So it wasn't Liverpool's fault, I just had to get out of there, find somewhere else.

The university café in London wasn't much different. But the speed of life, the fact there's always something to look at, diverted my thoughts for a while. I didn't speak to my parents much for the first few weeks. They were busy trying to stop Cress from becoming a dancer or a president or something they didn't want. And I would think about Dad's enormous frame blocking all the light in the doorway as yet another of Cress's suitors came to give his best offer. You could just make them out, if you strained and bent your body away from the kitchen table and looked down the hall. It used to make me laugh, Dad would always get the door before Cress made her entrance down the stairs like Shirley Bassey. And they would always have a little chat before the boy came into the house. I don't know what Dad said to them, but it seemed to work. They would come into the kitchen and blink a lot and gulp down Mum's disgusting home-made lemonade like it was their last supper. *Yes, Mrs Walker. Fine thanks, Mr Walker.* I miss Cress.

The therapist looks at me funny. You can get all this stuff for free at university. I'd finished my photography project for the term so I went to see if I could get some more funding from the college. I got a load of leaflets and one of them was for free counselling for students. I handed in my project – pictures of the political posters up around town, ready for the general election. It seemed to rain a lot for April, and the posters were reflected in the puddles on the street. I called it 'reflecting politics', handed it in and thought I was a genius. Didn't make any difference; the bloody grey man won again.

The therapist was young. He couldn't have been more than in his early thirties. He was really cool – I would have imagined something very different. He asked me how I found it, living away from home. I said I didn't find it hard at all. He asked me why I transferred in my first week, and I couldn't really give him an answer. I just needed to leave *something*, somewhere. I told him I could heat up baked beans and make toast and I had no complaints. So then we just had a chat for half an hour. And then I came back the next week and we had another chat. Not therapy: just a chat. He reminded me of the osteopath.

I'm telling him some funny things about Cress and he stops me in mid-sentence.

'Marlow, your sister . . .'

'Yes.'

'You obviously get on well with her.'

'I suppose so.'

'You, have you, do you have a girlfriend currently?'

'No.'

'May I ask when you last had a girlfriend?'

'Um, a while ago?'

'A month, a year?' he says calmly, smiling.

'Well, I've never had a long-term girlfriend. But I went out with girls at school.'

'What kind of girls do you like?'

'Chocolate ones,' I say.

He laughs, 'No, seriously.'

'I don't know if there's a type.' Then I start to describe Peri to him and he makes a couple of notes.

'Were you describing your sister there?' he says, again very calmly.

'No, no, I was describing a girl I like. Why would I describe my sister?'

He carries on. 'Does she have a name?'

'Peri.'

'And is she in London?'

196

'I don't know where she is. Why aren't we having a nice chat like normal?'

'There's no reason, Marlow. This is just an interesting angle to pursue. This isn't something which is dangerous or uncommon. Often a family member – perhaps one who is outstanding at something, or has appealing qualities, becomes a focus for a relative.'

'Okay . . . but I was talking about Peri.'

'Sure, I understand that. But just staying with your sister. Many boys find this when meeting girls for the first time. And in later life many men are really searching for someone to match their mother.'

'I'm not—'

'I know you're not. I just wonder whether you have your sister up on a pedestal.'

'I don't want to fuck my sister, Mark.'

'I know you don't,' he smiles, 'but families can be close and claustrophobic, and I wonder if your relationship with your sister should be less intense. At least from your side.'

'You're making me feel like a weirdo.'

'You're not a weirdo, Marlow. You just seem to have transferred something which usually concerns boys' mothers – and girls' fathers – onto your sister. You said yourself you didn't speak to anyone at school or your parents, so presumably all your focus during those years was on her.'

I think about that for an evening and go back the next day. I find out, along the way, that I got a D for my photography. Bollocks to that. Next time I'll get drunk beforehand.

'Mark?'

'Yes.'

'I'm not in love with my sister.'

'Marlow, you've told me a lot about yourself and in many of your stories, whether you realise this or not, there's a continuing theme.'

'And what's the theme?'

'One of protectiveness over her; one of thinking a little too highly of her.'

'I *do* feel protective of her.'

'But it's just protectiveness?'

I shrug, think about her standing, naked, dripping wet when I walked into the bathroom by mistake.

'Have you ever thought why that might be?' he says. I think about her breasts, her hips, her wet hair. I snap out of it. 'Because she's my sister. It's my job to kill people who hurt her.'

Mark looks shocked.

'I'm kidding, Mark. Don't worry, I'm kidding. I just thought we needed to lighten up.'

The sessions become more regular and the holidays start but I don't go home. I walk around the town in the morning, buy some cartridge paper to draw on, maybe go swimming in the afternoon, do a couple of thousand lengths, throw a few balls at some hoops at the indoor basketball court, meet some local players, don't talk to the other students much, then go and see Mark. I like him. He's easy to talk to; he isn't at all slimy. I tell him about my photography project, about the grey man's face reflected in a puddle and he thought it was great. He could see genius, too. I like that in a therapist.

'Was there ever a moment, perhaps when you were young, or maybe more recently, when something happened to your sister. Something which upset the family?'

'What, like her falling in a pond?'

'Bear with me. Try and think.'

'I don't know. Well, when she was small she was a real anarchist, she would do what she pleased.'

'And was there a particular time?'

'Not really. Not that I can think of.'

'Never a time when she was in danger . . .'

'Well, she wandered off once, when we were on holiday. She managed to open the front door of our apartment and she disappeared for a while.'

'What had happened?'

'She'd befriended a local kid, the son of the shop-keeper, and they were hoarding lollipops.'

'Is this true?' he smiles.

'Of course it's true.'

'But she came back all right?'

'She was fine. She hadn't been gone that long, although I remember my mother being very upset.'

'And your dad, how did he react?'

'He was a news reporter then. He was under a lot of stress.'

'Any other incidents?'

'Why is this of interest?'

'I was wondering if there was a moment, perhaps involving you and her, when you let her down, or when you felt that you could have helped stop something unpleasant happening to her. Perhaps something that

199

isn't in your conscious, but is lodged, nagging at you from your unconscious.'

'Oh. Okay.'

'But what happened on holiday doesn't really qualify as that,' he says, closing his notes for this session. 'What do you think?' he says, standing up.

19.

A DAY IN THE LIFE OF GORAN IVANISEVIC

We're halfway through 1992, and no one has asked me to speak any French or do any business. I wonder if there was anything at school that was any use. June is hot, but I don't see much of it as I spend most days watching Wimbledon on television. I'm transfixed by this Croatian player who's 6′ 4″ and is beating everyone in his path. I'm nearly as tall as him. He disappears under a towel when they change ends and mutters to himself. I have to watch all his matches, and it cuts into my life. In the end he nearly wins the tournament, but is knocked out by an American with long hair whom everyone loves. I've never seen anyone put their heart into something like Goran does.

Then the strangest thing happened. It had been years since Mum handbagged the man in the chemists who asked if Cress was a model. Cress had, of her own accord, in the summer holidays, come to London by herself for a day and got signed on the spot. They called Mum on the phone while Cress was in the office; they had her on the speaker phone, and the whole office could hear her going insane and telling her daughter off, oblivious to the open-plan office, all enjoying the drama. After a while, Dad's voice was audible on the phone, and then my mother and father had an argument while the employees of Total Modelling Agency, W1 listened to this domestic war in the commuter belt. After much negotiating, and Mum, and then Dad, coming up to London, they decided to let her, on the condition that any money she made, she didn't have any fun with. I didn't know about any of this at the time. I went to concerts, protests, pubs. I liked to keep busy. I joined a drawing class and the art teacher liked me with my charcoal, making large scrawls on the milky-coloured paper. I shouted about the way they gave internal examinations to female immigrants coming in to the airport. I wrote letters to everyone in public life who made me angry. Those were the things I enjoyed. I made some friends that I knew I would never keep, and went out with women whose names I could not tell you now. I had two relationships, each lasting one month, during which I wasn't sober for a single moment. And I always finished them before we had sex. And that was the only time I drank. Two months. I never really got into it.

Some days, like today, I go on trips to take photographs – nearly always unsuccessful as I'm too shy to just take pictures of people in the street. I mean, you take a picture of someone with a strange face in the street and everyone thinks you're brilliant. I'm worried that the person with the strange face is going to come after me. I'm walking around, trying to hide around corners and sneak pictures of people, when I see a flyer for Joel's band. They're playing at another university Union. It's still only afternoon but I go down there and sit in the bar. Sure enough, there's Joel and a bunch of misfits unloading gear from a truck. When Joel sees me, he swaggers over all casual, but I know he's really excited about it.

'Heard about us up in town then?'

'Yeah, I saw a poster in the bin; it'd been used to pick up dogshit,' I say.

By the time the band get on stage I feel drunk and I know I'm going to regret it. I don't feel well. Drink doesn't like me very much.

The band are good. Joel sings, well, shouts lyrics with real feeling. He and his lead guitarist exchange violent words from time to time. The band don't appear to like each other very much. After they've come off stage Joel walks around being a rock star for a bit, then comes and finds me and he drinks beer and I drink water. We talk about Marxism.

Then the shit hits the fan. A magazine hires Cress to be on their cover. It isn't like *Vogue* or anything, but you can get it in the newsagents. It's a sort of fashion and lifestyle magazine. But the photo is what causes the fuss, taken by a young up-and-coming photographer who wants to make his mark. And he does. It was the first cover of its kind on a magazine. It is Cress, sitting, facing away from the camera, with her back arched, her knees pulled up into her chest and her head resting on her arms which are wrapped around her knees. Oh, and she is naked. So I'm just about to go round to the editor's office with a gun when I remember what Mark said. So I just take a knife. Just joking. I don't do anything. I phone Dad.

'What d'you think?'

'Well, it's beautiful, I suppose,' Dad says. 'I wish she had some clothes on, but at least people can only see her back. She says that she had some underwear on, which they airbrushed out. What did you think?'

'It was okay. Is she there?'

'Hold on.' I can hear him call her, then I hear her shout at him as he tries to steal the sandwich she's eating. She comes to the phone.

'Hello brother,' she says.

'Why're you stripping off for dirty magazines?'

'What did you think?'

'It was great,' I say, reluctantly.

She takes a gasp-breath. '*Really?*' I can hear her smile. 'You know it's based on a painting. One by Picasso. *What one is it, Dad?*' she shouts to him.

'It's called Blue Nude,' he mumbles.

'And the photographer is going to enter it into some competitions,' she says. 'There's been all this fuss.'

'Because?'

'No one's had someone facing the wrong way on a cover before.'

'And what about your A levels?'

'Fuck them,' she says. 'I want to be a dancer.' I can hear Dad's voice tell her not to swear.

'I'm applying to some dance schools in London. I'll be coming up for auditions and you're taking me to Madame Tussauds.'

'I don't even know where that is.'

'Don't you go there all the time? I would.'

'What?'

204

'I'm joking, Marlow. God, you take everything so seriously. I'll send you a copy of the picture.'

'What picture?'

'The one of me.'

'What am I supposed to do with it?'

'Worship it,' she says.

6'4"

20.

0.1 DEGREES FROM NORMAL

Like a recurring nightmare, like rust which is the only thing holding a broken object together, Peri comes back.

I pass most things at college, I don't get kicked out, my grades get better. I try not to appear surprised. I have a small diversion when Goran Ivanisevic nearly wins Wimbledon again, but this time he's knocked out by a boring American with short hair. When I support a sports person, my commitment is total. I didn't support Brazil but they still won the World Cup. The only thing that gets in the way of Wimbledon is Lourdes and who will be the next leader of the Labour Party after John Smith died.

Lourdes. A drive-through McDonald's in London. I'm on my way to my flat; she's in front of me, in the queue. I watch her as she orders a strawberry milkshake. The waitress taking the order asks her if she wants a large one and she thinks about that for a minute.

'Large. Yes. And I wan' to eat a *borrgrre*,' she says in a thick accent.

'A what?'

'A *borrgrre*,' she repeats. The waitress points to a quarter pounder and Lourdes nods. The burger is put down in front of her, then the milkshake.

'The *Manayjorr* . . .' Lourdes says.

'I'm sorry?' the waitress says.

'The *Manayjorr* . . .' she says.

'What? You want to see him?'

Lourdes nods. The waitress scurries off behind the serving hatches, thinking if someone wants to see the manager after ten p.m. there's about to be gunfire. She looks worried. She doesn't want to get shot on those wages. And die wearing those clothes. What kind of medals are those to be buried in – a three-star McDonald's badge. A man walks towards us. He's wearing a suit, his tie loosened around his neck, the top button of his shirt undone. The waitress asks me what I want to eat. I find myself ordering the same as her. I look to my left.

'Hello Lourdes,' the manager says. 'I thought you'd handed your notice in.'

Lourdes takes the lid off the milkshake, puts the straw on the table in front of her, and then proceeds to pour the whole milkshake over his head. The gloopy, semi-solid pink goo sits on his head for a second before running down his face and neck, like a pink alien devouring his face. He grimaces and walks away without saying anything. I'm still looking at Lourdes. She has short dark hair, some strands of red and orange dye still noticeable, and incredibly hooded eyes. It takes her half a day to blink. Her nose is crooked; the angle it chooses at the bridge increases its already extreme attitude. She's attractive in a bad photofit kind of way. She looks sleepy, and her eyes only get about halfway open most of the time. It must be such an effort, holding up eyelids like that.

210

'He make only me wear shortest skirt when I *wurrk* here . . . an' touch me,' she rolls her *r*s for half an hour. It passes the time. 'My friend say to pour shake onto his head.'

I smile at her, kind of give my approval. I walk out of the restaurant, into the darkness. I finish my burger and go to throw the milkshake into the bin.

'Hey!' I hear behind me. I look round. She is walking towards me.

'You want shake?' she asks, looking at the pink hell in a cup, which I'm holding like a bomb.

'Not on my head,' I say. 'You want it?'

She nods. I hold the cup out and she takes it quickly, like I might change my mind any minute. She sucks on the straw, almost laughing to herself as she applies so much pressure to get the stuff into her mouth her cheeks nearly cave in. She doesn't seem embarrassed.

'What's your name?' I ask, just for conversation.

'*Lordeshh*,' she says.

'Where you from?'

'*Lishboa*.'

I get on a night bus all the way back to my house, and she follows me. From then on we live together, no questions. It isn't a normal thing, I'll give you that. Lourdes can't really speak English very well at all. But over the time she spends in England – the hours, the days, the weeks, the months – she really manages to get a *lot* worse. Lourdes had lived in Spain for a long time, although she was from Lisbon. So she swallowed her words like she was chewing gum, then emitted them, full of Spanish r's. It was an incomprehensible and charming combination.

In the entire time we're together we don't ever ask each other about the weather, who's going to buy toilet rolls, what to eat that evening, what to watch on TV. Everything just happens. Or usually it just doesn't. I never find out anything more about her apart from that she left Portugal for Spain, then Spain for Holland, then she got bored telling me so we never got any further. She shrugged a lot, rolled pizzas up into a tube and ate them by hand. Short hair, full lips, perfect skin, stupid shoes, unpredictable. That's all I know.

Every time I look at her, and feel attracted to her, I hope that it's enough to erase Peri from my mind. But I can't do it. I don't kiss her for several weeks. I can't figure out if she's a lodger or a friend or what. And I'm happy with that. I'm not much for sex any more, really. After a while she gives me money for the rent so I figure she's just a lodger. She sleeps on the couch every night, watching late-night political discussion programmes which she doesn't understand. She smiles if a man is wearing a funny tie, even if he's talking about war or famine. She just blinks slowly, as the politicians and the journalists do their thing – privileged players of the same game. And still Lourdes watches the flickering blue light from the television in the corner of the room.

Every night, before going to bed, I give her a glass of water. It's the normal ritual. I got her one on the first night, so I get her one every night. She drinks it in one go, looking up at me while she gulps it down, the same as when she sucked the milkshake to death. When she finishes it, she hands me the glass, turns away, and falls asleep. Tonight I give her the water, same ritual, then go to bed. As I doze off I feel breathing by my face. I jump slightly, look up. Lourdes is kneeling down by the bed. I move over and she gets in. She moves up to me, I put an arm around her and we sleep. So we do that for a few days, then one night she comes to bed wearing nothing. She lies by me, closes her eyes. I move on top of her, kiss her. She opens her eyes. I move my hand between her legs and as I do, she reaches her mouth up to me to kiss me. Her right hand appears from under the duvet, holding a condom. I hold it in my hand, think for a second, then roll back onto my side of the bed. I want to shout, to finally scream Peri out of my head for good. I rest my hand on Lourdes's stomach. There isn't a word or a moment of awkwardness or a *'what are you thinking about?'* question.

A couple of times I'd be reading or drawing and she'd walk up and offer her bare wrist to me, holding a knife in the other hand. She'd say, 'Shall I cut myself?' – like she was asking me if I wanted a piece of toast. I'd say no and she'd put the knife away, and carry on with whatever she was doing before. Another day I came home and she'd bought a bumper pack of thermometers. She was sitting at the kitchen table, two thermometers in her mouth, one in each corner. She looked like a bug. She was holding a crystal up in front of her, like she was worshipping it. Another time I came home and I could hear she was being fucked in the bedroom. An hour or so later she and

213

a girl with a ring in her nose came out and watched TV with me.

People I knew had girlfriends who liked cats and buying shoes. My girlfriend worshipped crystals with multiple thermometers stuck in her. She said she wanted to stick a thermometer up her arse. I knew she wanted me to act surprised and try and stop her. So I let her do it. Everyone has to learn that one for themselves. They were the digital ones, she delighted in the fact they beeped when you set them. They would carry on beeping until they were cooked. She looked at the leaflet to find out what a human's normal temperature was. She was always .1 or .2 degrees away from normal. That was if you were being kind about it. The day her temperature came out exactly on the dot she gave out a little cheer. She showed me the readout proudly. You'd think she'd just weighed her soul.

When it was my birthday she gave me a beautiful series of prints of paintings. I put them up in my room and around the house. Then one of her weirdo friends came round the next day and walked round the flat and took them all down. I watched him as he did this. He said, 'Lourdes, why d'you always steal stuff from my house?'

She shrugged.

Then, finally, I wake up and Lourdes isn't next to me. Her clothes are scattered everywhere, but her crystals are no longer strewn across the floor. After a few days I receive six postcards which I'd bought and was saving to send to someone. I hadn't noticed they'd left my drawer. On the back, handwritten, are excerpts from

War and Peace. The postmark is Lisbon. That's the end of Lourdes. Another part of my life like Peri, comes and goes at will – entering and then leaving, crippling me.

My lectures for Monday are cancelled as one of the lecturers has sold a book and is doing a publicity tour. People are starting to get famous all over the place. It used to be only Grace Kelly that was famous. Now everyone is: gardeners, cooks, my lecturer. I get up early anyway and buy a packet of those envelopes with the little see-through window on the front. Then, on the computer at college, I put on Peri's name and her parents' address. Above it, I design a logo for a fictional company. On the outside of the envelope I print *Important*. Inside, though, is a handwritten letter to her.

Two mornings later, the phone wakes me up before nine.

'That was pretty clever, Marlow,' Peri says.

'I know.'

'My parents forwarded it to me; they thought it was the lottery or something.'

'We haven't spoken for a while,' I say.

'I know, how've you been? What're you up to?' she says, brightly. Unnaturally so.

'Well, I'm in . . . who cares what I'm doing, where the fuck are you, and why do you keep disappearing? Do you think it's enigmatic?'

'Nice word.'

'Well?'

'It's difficult,' she says.

215

'It's always difficult with you. But you make it that way. Actually it's simple.'

'I'm coming to London soon.'

'Good. Well why don't you give me a call if you can be fucked and we'll go and see a musical.'

'Sarky fucker. Okay, I'll see you tomorrow. You get the tickets.'

'Tomorrow?'

'Yeah.'

'So you're coming down tomorrow? When did you decide this?'

'When I got your letter this morning.'

'But you said you were coming to London soon, like you had something to do here.'

'I do. See you.'

21.

WHAT WAS PERI LIKE?

She looks behind me when I open the door, I'm not sure what she's looking for. She follows me into the sitting room. There's that moment when people make a comment about the flat, or the weather, or something. But Peri doesn't ever do that.

'I'll have a cup of coffee, then,' Peri fumbles in her pocket for a cigarette. She lights it and I go into the kitchen.

'Whose clothes are these?' she shouts.

'Oh, this girl.' I say.

'Your girlfriend?'

'No.'

I walk back in, have a good look at Peri. I realise that for someone who's been on my mind so much, I never had a clear picture of what she looked like. Her image in my head was always more than her appearance. Her hair is quite dark now; maybe she has dyed it. Her skin doesn't look like it's been made-up; it looks too smooth. But her voice is sharp and edgy, with an efficiency which few people have. She talks briefly about visiting an aunt in Australia: sun and wide open spaces – they'll cure anything that trees and Scotland don't. After the incident in the Paradise Arcade, when she and I went down there, she had a bit of a breakdown. Those were her words. I mean, what's a *bit* of a breakdown? *A bit of an apocalypse.*

'Thought about being a masseur,' she says.

'Why would you want to do that?'

'I dunno, had a massage the other day . . . was pretty good.'

'Uh huh.'

'I lay there, after she finished. Then I cried,' she says. Her stilted speech is contagious.

'That a good thing?'

'Uh huh.'

The room goes darker and then lighter as clouds pass quickly overhead, blocking out the sun. I don't move from my seat; I don't even move in my seat. I just sit there, transfixed by her talking. Some people from my course are crashing at my flat, and helping to pay the rent since Lourdes left. They come back and chat away with Peri and me.

'Who's *that!*' one of them says, as I go upstairs to get my jacket.

'A friend.'

'She's never a student'

'Yeah.'

'She's gorgeous. Looks foreign.'

We sit in a twenty-four hour café.

'So I know that you've been doing some therapy and taking some courses, and spending time where there's no one from your past and lots of trees . . .'

'Yeah . . .' she says.

'But what I still haven't understood is why you cut

everything off from me. Why you swooped back and then disappeared again.'

'Dunno. I wanted to get away. So I left.'

'That's it?'

'Well, I can give you a breakdown of all the places I went, if you want?' she says, sarcastically. 'All the crappy jobs I did.'

'I really felt something for you.' I say it in the past tense for no reason.

'Well, it wasn't really the best grounds for a relationship, was it?'

'So what did you do?'

'After the arcade?'

'Yeah.'

'I did my A levels. Well, I studied for them at home. I got them. I nailed my history teacher. He was only thirty-five. Then I started college but dropped out. Then I just kept enrolling at different places and dropping out. Saw my aunt for a bit.'

We walk back to my house. When we get there, the others are in bed. They've left the television on, playing silently in the background.

'You want a massage?' Peri asks. I lie down on the sofa. I take my top off. She asks me where I keep the towels. I take my trousers off and lie on my stomach. She puts a towel over my legs and backside. She rummages in a little bag of hers and gets out some oils. I lie under her hands. When she's finished, I get a headache and a brief feeling of anger – I don't know what about. After a while it goes. I sit up, feel a little dizzy.

We go to bed. When I wake up, Peri isn't beside me but

I know she hasn't disappeared. Her clothes are draped over my chair, her silver bracelet is on the window ledge. All these student houses have bad insulation and a smiley face has been finger-painted in the condensation on the window. I can hear bath water flowing away. The door opens and she comes back in, with two of my towels around her.

'I'm having a bath,' she says.

'Are you going today?'

'I was going to . . .'

'Stay for a while,' I say. I get out of bed and walk over to her. As I stand up, she looks up at me. We kiss and it's the most loaded, volatile kiss – a tiny connection with so much history, so many different faces we've both had over the years, now merged into our present states. The kiss goes on, and when it ends we don't know what to do. Downstairs my new flatmates are cooking breakfast for everyone. There's tension between us. I've noticed it in other people – this is the first time I've noticed it in myself. I'm surprised laser beams aren't shooting out of my head and into Peri's.

'You talk to your parents much?' Peri asks, as we sit in another café in town later on.

'A bit. Not that much. You?'

'Hardly ever. They did their best, which was shit. I don't hold anything against them but I've got nothing to say to them. Drug-addled fools. Your sister all right?'

'She's moving to London soon. Gonna be a model.'

'A model? My God. Her and Lucy – I thought they'd be a double act of some sort.'

'Well, she wants to be a dancer, so she's doing this first to get some money.'

'Why are you staring at me so hard?'

'You know how perverse it was, what we did in the arcade.'

She dismisses it with a shrug. 'I'd just loved to have seen my parents' faces if they knew. I think that beats their wife-swapping.'

'Did you lose your virginity that night, Peri?'

'Sure felt like it,' she says, looking down, making me feel bad or guilty.

'No I mean . . .'

'I know what you mean. Yes. And you did too.'

'How do you know I did too? I could have—'

'No you couldn't.'

'I like your bracelet,' I say.

'It's my grandmother's. She used to live in some Eastern European country where it snows all year round and gets invaded once a week.'

'Maybe you have some of her in you.'

'What do you mean?' she scowls.

'Nothing. You just look a bit . . .'

In my room she is kneeling up on the bed, her naked legs folded under her. I lean towards her and kiss her. I push her backwards, and she falls slowly back onto the bed. I kiss her neck. I put my hands on the bottom of her shirt and move it up her body. She puts her arms up so I take it off, over her head. With one hand she starts to undo my trousers. I kneel up and look down at her, look at a woman's body. So this is what Prince has been

221

singing about all these years? This must be what it's like to want someone so much you'll do anything.

Her eyes are closed for a moment.

I take her knickers off, and she flicks them expertly with her left foot so they fly onto the floor. I move my face between her legs, look up her body. Her hands cup my face affectionately then fall back by her side. I move my face closer and kiss, and gently lick and slowly let my lips and tongue wander. She's absolutely quiet for a while. I wonder if I'm really any good at this. I never gave it much thought before: that you could be good or bad at it. Before it was just the fact that you *were* doing it at all. The brown-blonde hairs between her legs get damp as I press my mouth harder against her. I can feel her shaking a little. When she comes, I kneel back up. I leave one hand resting between her legs, and I can feel the heat – nothing like normal body heat; this is a focused, direct heat – which is coming from her.

The flies on my jeans are pointing out at an unbelievable angle so, as she lies there, I take them off, slip on a condom, then get back into the same position. I lie on top of her and kiss her. She takes my penis and rubs it against her which feels muted but then makes me gasp when I push into her. Our mouths twist against each other. She puts her hands on my back as I push into her, my mouth on hers the whole time. The skin on our stomachs is rubbing so hard, I'm waiting for a fire to start. I swell that little bit just before I come, but I keep on pushing in and out of her until my eyes feel like they're facing the wrong way around, like they're pointing into my head rather than out of it.

Afterwards we lie on the bed: her head is at the top resting on the pillow; my head at the foot of the bed. Our legs are arched up and intertwined. It's the most relaxed I ever remember being.

I dream I'm naked inside a warm, wet room – the walls soft with a liquid gel running down them. It's funny what your brain comes up with while you are asleep – when your foot falls off the side of the bed, you have a little dream about falling off a curb; when I wake up with my penis in her mouth that's the best my mind can do. I stretch my arms above my head and close my eyes as I feel Peri's mouth tight around me. Her tongue flicks in and out like a snake, her reptile eyes look up at me as I cough and splutter and her expression changes little as I get more into it. She moves up to my face, the weight of her body like a protective layer. But she's as distant as I am close. When she kisses me, it tastes of me in her, back in me again. And I know that she'll never love me, or even give me anything like part of her. She isn't reachable.

'Have you ever been in love with anyone?' she asks.

'I'm not sure,' I lie. 'Have you?'

'I never could be. I've never even felt close to it.'

223

22.

THE OTHER GIRL

'I miss London,' Dad says, tucking into his lunch like he's never been fed. He looks out the window at the manic streets as if he's looking at a lover. He gazes longingly at the pollution.

'I don't know why we ever moved,' he says. 'I miss this city. Anyway, how's everything? How's your course?'

'I don't know if I'm much for photography.'

'Now's the time to work that out. Just give it a decent shot. If it doesn't work out, then think again about something else.'

'Why didn't Mum come up today?'

'She's busy. Got something on with some group in the village,' he says dismissively. 'I just dropped Cress off at her house.'

'By herself!'

'No, she's staying with a family I know from years ago. I said she had to stay there for a bit, and then if she still wanted to be in the city she could get a flat with her girlfriends.'

'What's she going to do?'

'I dread to think. I stuck the TV on the other day and she was dancing on an advert for The Gap. Must they show their belly buttons the whole time? I nearly had a heart attack,' he smiles, proudly. 'If she earns enough money to put herself through dance school, and I bet she bloody does as well,' he says, smiling, 'she'll deserve it. So although I'm not sure about the modelling, I think, good for her.'

The waitress takes away our plates. We order some pudding. Dad has put on a little weight, but he looks well. His skin always looks healthy and weathered, and his cheeks have fattened slightly. His hair is short, and looks like he has just got out of bed: a brown-blond mess.

'I'm so proud of you and your sister. I think you're both wonderful.'

'Well, um, thanks ... that's nice. Thing is, this might not be the best time to tell you this, but there's something ...'

'What?' he asks, eyeing the apple strudel that has been put in front of him.

'Can I just say this straight.'

'Yes,' he says.

'Well, you know, I know about what happened in the arcade.'

Dad looks into his strudel, into the glowing yellow custard, as if it will give him the answer. He shakes his head.

'How do you know?' he says, his voice low and stern. He doesn't look up.

'Well, it's pretty obvious now.'

'How is it obvious? Sorry, wait, *how* can you know? I don't understand?' he says, like he's fighting with himself.

'I know about the arcade, I know what happened.'

226

Dad looks angry. 'I don't think you know what you're talking about. There's no way you could know—'

'Dad, I'm telling you—'

'What do you know?' he says quickly, angrily.

'I know that she was taken, and I know that her parents don't think she knows.'

'Her parents? Well, *we* are sure she doesn't know.'

'Eh?'

'Marlow, you know all the details?'

'Yes. I know all the details.'

'You know she was taken, she was sexually assaulted. You know that?' Dad is almost crying, anger in his voice subsiding.

'She wasn't assaulted. They got her, the security people got her.'

'No, son. That's not true.'

'It is. I promise. I know, I've spoken to her.'

'You've spoken to Cress about this!' He leans forward, like he's going to kill me.

'Cress?' I say.

'Yes.'

'Peri . . .'

Somewhere, outside of this café, the city feels huge, like the metropolis it is. In the café the walls are closing in, my head is tightening, throbbing.

'Cress,' Dad says. 'She's the other girl.'

People come and go. Someone gets told they have to eat something if they want to sit down. The coffee machines blot out the radio from time to time. Dad doesn't take his eyes off me. If we lost contact we might not find our way back. He stands up, motions for me to do the same. My head is spinning, I feel sick. Dad puts a tenner on the table and, with his arm around me, walks quickly out of the café. He stands in front of a cab, stops it. We get in. He gives an address.

'Where, where we going?' I say. I feel like I'm shrinking, becoming unnoticeable again. I'm choking.

'Gran's house,' he says, roughly, his arm around me.

We get there and Dad unlocks the door. My mind is contorting, twisting and nothing is coming out. I've not registered anything since we were in the café. Dad takes a couple of beers out of the fridge. We talk very quickly, and say odd things, like you do after a car accident.

'Granny One drinks beer?'

'They're mine.'

'How'd they get in here?'

'I come here quite often.'

'To London?'

'Just me. By myself. Come and sit here in the quiet if your gran is away. Look after the flat. Water the plants.'

'They didn't assault her, Dad. They didn't. They didn't . . .' I can feel my throat swelling, the tears are pouring down my face. I can feel my stomach pulse, contract. I throw up. I can hear screaming and only on a delay, like a transatlantic phone conversation, do I realise that it's me.

We've stayed two days in Gran's house. We've slept in the same room. He still hasn't taken his eyes off me.

'You know when I left journalism. When you were at school.'

228

'Yes.'

'Why did you think I did that?'

'Didn't like the stress of it.'

'Well, that's about ten per cent of the answer.'

We sip our drinks. Two men. And Dad tells me that he nearly split up with my mother at that time. He nearly split up with her because she was asking him to do something which he didn't agree with. But he gave in, did what she asked, and it ate away at him, ate away his insides until he was just guilt and ulcers.

'She didn't want to tell you. She took the advice of a doctor – in her defence, that kind of medicine has come a long way since then – and she did, *we* did, the wrong thing. I remember the feeling of knowing you weren't okay, but not being able to help you, not being together enough myself, to be any use to you – Cress was on my mind and I couldn't think clearly about anything else.' I finish my beer, put it down, shakily. I can hear Sausage's voice saying, *It made me frightened.* And Mum's reaction on the day we were shopping and the alarm went off, that she was so upset and angry with herself. A cacophony of alarms starts, each overlapping the other in my head.

'You always knew this, didn't you, Marlow?' Dad says, softly.

'I don't know.' I'm breathless.

'I think inside, you did. You two are so close. There's something in you that recorded the disruption to the family. Even if you don't actually remember it. That's why you are the way you are with her.'

Later, we sit in the room and the silence is the only

229

thing left which is protecting me. Dad goes into the kitchen and makes some food. I can see a curly straw in there, made from plastic and covered in tiny shining gold stars, which Cress used to use to drink her disgusting milkshakes with. When we came to stay with Gran, Cress would put both chocolate and strawberry powders in the bottom, and then fill it up with milk. Everywhere there are memories which all say the same thing: *you could have stopped it.*

I stuff the cottage pie into my face quickly. I don't feel like eating anything.

'Cress doesn't even have a clue?' I say.

'We're certain she doesn't. There were signs. I mean, her behaviour – she was a great child . . . but there were things . . .' he tails off, tries to stop himself from crying.

'What things?'

'She was exploring sex earlier. She's chosen a career showing off her body. Her sexuality came out strongly and very early.'

'And with me, I sometimes thought she was . . .'

'What?'

'Nothing,' I say.

'But then lots of girls are models, and girls become aware of their sexuality at different ages.' Dad gives up, his voice trails off. 'I dunno, did we do the right thing?'

I don't answer that. I think about her putting her hand on my lap, the ironic smile she gave me when she came out of the shower. *If I wasn't your sister you'd want me, wouldn't you?*

'But with Peri,' I start, 'I mean, that's insane that *two*

230

girls are both—' I stop when I see how Dad is looking at me. He watches my mind catch up, trying to believe what he's going to say.

'We took advice from people, from doctors. They said perhaps if Peri and Cress were allowed to mix socially from an early age they would be able to determine if either of them had knowledge of what had happened. Particularly for Cress, she was younger, it was important to not put her through pain in later life if it wasn't necessary.'

'So we were an experiment.'

'You weren't. Cress and Peri were. We were trying to cause them both the least amount of pain. It didn't work because you and Peri got on so well – probably because you were the displaced one at that time, because of school, and not Cress. So you two were drawn together in a way we expected her and Cress to be. We asked a lot of people, but we had as little a clue as anyone. We got some ridiculous suggestions. Mrs Mottished was a psychiatrist, so she would observe. That's why they were around the whole time. We had other people come round to observe, but I don't think anyone truly knew what they were doing. How could they?'

I shake my head, my eyes smarting.

'I know you resent me, and I understand, Marlow, I do. And it's as much my fault as it is your mother's.'

'Why would I resent you?'

'I spent so much time away. I couldn't be there to help you at school, because of work. I *asked* to be put on foreign stories – I couldn't stand my entire life becoming centred around one horrific incident. But not knowing how you and Cress were turning out, not seeing you for months on end. Then, when I came back, me and your mother would fight. She felt I'd just come back, criticise and then leave again.

'I don't know what to say.'

'Your mother was even advised by the doctor that bone manipulation and even the free chat with a young man might stimulate your mind into remembering things. And she didn't want to add you into the mix.'

'But I could have had that at school. Kids talk about loads of stuff.'

'But you weren't, were you? You weren't talking to anyone there.'

'Well, that's a dodgy theory.'

'I agree. But you know, it's different, for your mother, after Cress . . . you know . . . she knew straight away that she would never be the same. We were both changed, but she thought I was selfish because, eventually, I wanted to carry on with life. We still had our girl, for Christ's sake. Some people lose everything. She thought me stopping work was just an excuse. She didn't realise how ill it had made me, all the lies.'

I catch a glimpse of us both in the mirror – we look similar. We stay at the house for another night. The last time we spent real time together, I dragged him on a canoeing holiday and we stayed in tents by a river. He would cook noodles for supper over a knackered old gas stove. They were the best noodles ever, of course, because they were cooked by him. We canoed in the morning then went to the beach in the afternoon. I remember the dark, disgusting-looking beer he would have for lunch. And he would always have a plough-man's so I did too, even though I preferred chips with something. We met people who had the time to stand around and tell you the story of their lives. One evening, we were canoeing down some fairly mild rapids when I capsized and couldn't get out. I was struggling, my head underwater, the canoe upside down. I stayed relaxed as I'd been taught to, but then something snagged onto the deck of the canoe. A strap from my life jacket had caught. I remember the feeling of total force with which I was held by the water, and then by a greater, more majestic force as my father's hands grabbed me and pulled me from the canoe and up into the light and oxygen. I was so short I couldn't even stand up in the water. He held me with one arm and waded, steadying himself against the occasional rocks, as he navigated the slippery surface on the bottom of the river, me under his arm like a package.

'What d'you want for breakfast?' he asks.

'Anything,' I say. Dad is wearing a bathrobe; his hair is wet. I go into the bathroom. I wash with Gran's disgusting scented soap – she's away on a coach trip to France with thousands of women who all look like pepper pots – and remember that Peri is still at my house, and she's probably wondering where I am. And then I remember that she's Peri and that she wouldn't wonder. I can still taste her kiss in my mouth, in my pulse. I get out of the shower, look around me – everything Granny owns is pink. Or smells pink. I go back downstairs.

'Your breakfast is in the oven,' he says. 'I hope

233

you eat well in London; you've got a lot of space to fill.'

'I do eat well.'

It was that little moment of concern of his that was the thread, that you can still care about the small things, that you can still care at all, whatever happens. And whatever happens in the future, I'll always like being with the man who's sitting there, eating his eggs on toast.

'You all right today, Marlow?' he says.

'No,' I exhale, then try a smile.

234

23.

THE CLUB

'Hello,' Peri says, as I walk in.

'I've been away for a few days.'

'I know.'

'Don't you want to know where I've been?'

'Do you want to tell me?'

I look at her hard face, walk out the door, get the bus to college. I stop off on the way and call Mark from a phone box.

'Hi Marlow,' he says, when I walk in to his room. 'Haven't seen you for a while.'

I start telling him a censored version of events. I just tell him Cress was taken, but recovered straight away. He looks in shock, he really does. It's strangely comforting – I don't think I could have carried on talking to him if he hadn't reacted. We talk for a while. Then I ask him about the memory thing.

'Children remember things before they have language. They just record them in their guts. That stays there forever. Even when they *do* have language it's often too late to decipher because those emotions were programmed into you when you didn't have any analytical framework. So that affects how you remember things, and what you can recall in later life.'

'So, does she know? Like in some weird unconscious way?'

'I remember you telling me your sister calls your father by a name that only your mother uses. Things like that do often happen because of a disruption. She was formulating language, learning to speak, and there was that large disruption in her life. Sometimes it comes out as a learning deficiency which rights itself; sometimes it's something which is inexplicable, a strange detail.'

'Well,' I say. 'Thanks, Mark.'

He changes the subject slightly. 'You wanted to protect her.'

'Yes.'

I walk back from our session. Mark tells me to come back whenever I need to. He gives me a home number to call.

'Where've you been?' Peri says when I walk back into my house.

'Nowhere special,' I say and burst out into nervous laughter which soon becomes just nervous shaking. I tell her everything. For while she just shakes her head, her eyes are glazed over, almost changing colour to an aged yellow as she takes in what I'm saying. She sits down like she's about to faint. Her hardness suits this situation; she looks like she was built for these kind of things; she seems in her element. It looks right on her.

'Did you ever have an idea that it was Cress? The other girl,' I say.

'No. It's not like you join a club,' she says, evenly.

'No, I just thought . . .'

'How are we going to tell her?' Peri doesn't wait for

236

me to answer. 'Or, d'you think she knows and isn't letting on?'

'Not everyone is a clever as you.'

'She's clever. Is your Dad going to say anything?'

'Fuck, I don't know. It's not like he's just found out. He known for ages and hasn't said anything. I don't know if I can just *do* anything now. She's doing so well, she's earning more money at nineteen than any of us. I can't just walk up to her and fuck her life up like that.'

Peri looks at me.

'*Can I?*' I say, waiting for her to tell me that I can't.

'Yes, you can. You *have* to. If it'd just come out in the open for me a long time ago there wouldn't have been all this bullshit, all this fabrication.'

'I'm not sure how she'd react, you know. How would anyone react. Fuck, I can't even think about it without throwing up. It's like her idea of protecting parents will be shattered in one go. All the stability you thought you had, your grounding, just isn't there any more.'

I wake up in the middle of the night. Peri is sitting at my desk, naked.

'Peri? You all right?' She doesn't turn round, or even register. 'Peri!' I say, pushing the covers away from me. I get out of bed, walk towards her. I lean over, put a hand on her shoulder, expecting her to jump. She doesn't, she just looks round at me, tears in her eyes, a broken little face looking up at me, terrified and alone, confused and distant. I put my hand under her arms and motion for her to get out of the chair. She stands up, her slender body

237

against mine and I put my arms around her, walk her back into bed. I look over to the desk. There's a piece of paper on there now covered in doodles. Smiling faces in thick pencil are everywhere. We get back into bed, and she just turns away from me and lies there. She doesn't sleep, her breathing doesn't change. When I wake in the morning she's at my desk again, mindlessly looking at its surface.

'I'm going to see Cress,' she says.

6′ 5″

24.

GOLD STARS

I drop Cress off, have a quick tour of her new flat, then bring the car back. The Aretha Franklin song still rings in my ears, interrupted only by the half-hourly news reports on Nick Leeson and the bank. Something is rattling in the car, and it brings back the sounds of the camera shutter firing off. Spending today at the modelling shoot just made it more difficult – she was so pleased to see me. I think about the easy chat we had as I drove back, listening to the radio. On the passenger seat she's dropped the picture I drew on the back of a receipt. As I look at it, I'm still relieved that Peri has not yet gone through with her threat.

It's dark when I get in. I walk into the bathroom while Peri is in the bath. She screams. On the tray, where soap usually goes, there are several capsules – anti-depressants. She turns round, sees me looking at her.

'Did you tell her?'

'No.'

'If you don't I *will*,' she spits, and turns back round.

I go out to work; I do security work sometimes. I look into those grainy monitors and try and lose my thoughts in the grey. When I get back in the early morning Peri is passed out, not asleep, on the bed. Bottles of drink, and the general debris of trying-to-forget litter the room. I don't wake her, get back in my flatmate's car and drive over to Cress's. I want to call Dad but something is stopping me. Perhaps Peri's threat isn't real. I walk into Cress's flat. When I see the threatening red light blinking on her answer machine in her living room my short upswing in mood ends. The little display full of dread. There are six thousand messages on the answer machine for her. She sees me looking.

'Oh, I didn't see those.' She presses the play button. My heart jumps when I hear a voice which could be Peri's, but it's her sister Lucy. Cress ignores all of the messages apart from Lucy's, and picks the phone up straight away to call her. I go into the other room, banging my head on the beam.

'Mind the beam,' Cress says, laughing. I drink a glass of water. My lips are dry and chapped. Cress is still on the phone, and I lie on the floor, try to straighten my back out. Cress says goodbye and hangs up.

'Marlow, Lucy is going mad.'

'Why?'

'Well, I don't know, she wants to come over. Why're you lying on the floor?'

'My back.'

'You should go to my osteopath.'

'Make an appointment for me,' I say.

'You're a lazy shit, my boy. Are you gonna stay round while Lucy comes over?'

'I was hoping to stay a bit longer?'

'How long?'

'Indefinitely? I've moved out of my flat,' I lie. I think of Peri there, bottles of alcohol tangled in the sheets of the bed, cigarettes and dirty clothes. I think of Peri phoning Lucy, telling her she'd just arrived back in town. And now Lucy has phoned Cress, setting off a chain of events.

'Why do you need to stay here?' she says.

'I can't remember. Can I stay?'

'I thought you found some flatmates.'

Now she's having difficulty. She has her own flat – and likes her privacy. She has this idiosyncrasy: if someone is in the house then she has to make some kind of an effort. She makes an effort all day for a job and she doesn't want to have to do it when she comes home. She's biting her lip and frowning while she thinks, which makes her look like a little girl. I feel my throat tighten.

'Well, you can stay for a bit,' she smiles.

'I'll grow on you,' I offer.

'Like a fungus,' she says. I figure if I spend enough time with her, I can tell her, or stop Peri telling her; either way I can lessen the effect.

Cress dials a number and makes me an appointment for early evening at the osteopath. I haven't seen Lucy for many years. In my mind she's still the little girl who would come round to be with me so Cress and Peri could bond. But Cress and Lucy have been best friends their whole lives, and I still remember vividly how they used to narrowly avoid causing national incidents when they were young—picking up the phone and dialling random numbers, their planning and scheming, dancing to Aretha Franklin.

'D'you ever just chat?' Cress asks, breaking the silence.

243

The doorbell goes and she gets it. Lucy walks into the room. She looks round.

'Wow, this is great,' Lucy says. 'What about this for a first flat.'

Cress looks awkward; she's decorated it so it doesn't show off its wealth, but you just can't hide it completely.

'Could you imagine owning something like this when you were twenty, Marlow?' Lucy says.

'I can't imagine owning a banana.'

'Well, I'm getting a flatmate. A friend is moving in,' Cress says, humbly, as if she needs help with the rent.

Lucy sits down.

'So, how's everything?' Cress says, 'I haven't seen you for ages.'

'Well, guess what?'

'What?' Cress says. Cress would say 'Who's there?' if she was told a million 'knock, knock' jokes in a row. She has that female politeness; she'd laugh at your jokes just because she liked you.

'Peri's coming back,' Lucy says. I pretend to look surprised.

'Oh my God!' Cress says, excitedly. She looks at me, 'Did you hear—' She stops herself. I know she's only trying get me to take part. 'Wait, don't move,' she says running out of the room, 'I've got some things in the oven and some drinks – I want to hear all of this . . .' My back hurts. I can hear Cress in the kitchen. I can hear her dance, counting 'five, six, seven and . . .' to herself as she moves plates and food around. She's an entertainer. She loves people, animals, trees, grass, lipstick, strangers, cool shoes and anything else that life throws at her. And I'm about to fuck it all up. She has enough life in her for six people.

Lucy opens a magazine while she smokes. We have an arrangement: we're not interested in each other at all, so we just don't bother to talk. We like each other, but we don't pretend. I love people like that.

I think about my father, the look on his face when I last saw him.

'Are you going to tell her?' he asked, almost resigned – perversely glad? – that after years of only him and my mother knowing, someone else would now feel a responsibility. Now I would do as I wanted. I have Cress's happiness in my hands. But so does Peri.

I look at Cress: she looks nothing like my mother. I can't really see my mother anywhere in her face. And her personality is so different. I can only see my parents as two people who shouldn't have been together in the first place. They don't look right together. Some people start to look like their pets, others look like their spouses. My mother just looks more and more like herself every day. She has a rather imposing face and manner. She's always tanned and her dark hair is always cut into the kind of bob that has its own attitude. It's an impatient haircut. It curls under at the bottom so precisely that if you turned it upside down it would be a perfect bowl. She has a coldness which, now I know, only came after her child had been assaulted. She was never that way when I was very young. She was hardened and damaged by the experience. To my surprise, I now feel sorry for her. Her youth and sense of fun were just torn from her hands, plunging her into desperation. I've seen her enjoy herself from time to time since then. I *think* I can remember her enjoying herself. I thought my parents' connection was because they were both Londoners, but that was a false hope. They've never visited my flat. Or Cress's in St John's Wood. That's where Cress lives. Our parents told her she should invest her money, so she rented the most expensive flat she could find. Dad said they needed to have chat about what investment actually means. She'll probably buy it in a few years, anyway. I told them I would like to invest in something and they laughed.

Cress and Lucy are still hugging – it's quite sweet – both oblivious to the game Peri is playing. I grab a key and slip out of the room, holding the bit of paper with the osteopath's address on. I get on the tube, and one stop later I'm there. Within a few minutes I'm only wearing my boxer shorts and I'm lying on the table waiting for a strange man to come in the room, ask me all kinds of questions and then click my bones. This is routine for me. The man walks in: he's about my age, tanned forearms like all osteopaths, with a name that's so long it doesn't fit on his badge. He's wearing one of those smock tops; he could operate, paint a canvas, or give Communion.

'I didn't know it was that bad, Father,' I say. He looks at his white dog collar top on his smock and laughs. They always love that one.

'How many times have I heard that one?' he says dismissively.

'I thought I was the only one who ever said it.'

'Everyone says it,' he says. He looks a little tired. 'Have you been here before?'

'No, no, I haven't.'

'Have you been to an osteopath before?' he asks.

'Yes.'

'Roughly how many times?'

'In my life?'

'Yes.'

I huff and puff like you should when you're about to give a good answer.

'About a hundred,' I say.

'Really?' he says. 'So you must have had some real problems.'

'That's me,' I say.

'But you've not been to this practice before?'

'No, I've just moved to the area.'

'Oh, that's nice. When?'

'Twenty minutes ago,' I say. Knocking his questions back quickly protects me. It calms me knowing he can't get through to me.

'Right,' he says, like he wants to get on. He starts his business and I lie there, all limp. After a few minutes he starts the clicking, which is pretty successful. I can click on cue, any time. I'm their dream. He seems pleased with what's happening and he perks up again. The smell of the stuff they use to warm up your muscles hits me, reminds me of lying, a tiny child, on the upside-down see-saw on my first ever visit.

'You almost don't fit on this,' he says. 'So tall. So, did someone tell you about this place?'

247

'It was a recommendation. One of your patients, I think.'

'Oh, really. Who?'

'Cress Walker.'

He goes quiet for a second.

'You know her?' he asks.

'Yes.'

'That woman is . . . I'm the envy of the whole practice. Can you imagine, you graduate in September and the following year she's lying on your table. I've never seen . . . well, this might sound unprofessional.'

'Then don't say it,' I cut in.

'Sorry. It's just that you're a bloke and, I was just, you know. She's so. Well. So, you know her?'

'I'm her brother.'

Osteopath Antonopoulos is pretty quiet for the rest of our session. I wish he'd keep talking, because I can't stop thinking about Peri's ultimatum – which wasn't hers to give, – in the first place. Now I don't know whether I'm here on a damage limitation exercise or about to announce the end of the world. The end of Cress's little world, anyway. It's amazing how many things which aren't life-threatening can ruin you. It's not the fact that it's something you didn't know, it's the fact that it was hidden from you which hurts so much. And now I feel selfish for thinking about the Peri part of the situation, and not about Cress. When the supervisor comes in, quite a long time later, she asks me to stand up so she can look at my back.

'How tall are you?' she asks.

'Six five, I think.'

248

'And the rest of your family?'

'My sister is nearly six foot. My Dad is six two and my mother is a dwarf.'

'You're joking?'

'Yes.'

'Right,' she says. 'Did you have a sudden growth, or was it steady?'

'Slow, slow, quick, quick, slow,' I say. She traces a finger down my spine, writes some notes in her clip-board and she leaves. I put my clothes back on. Mr Antonopoulos wants to say something, I can tell. As I go to leave, he says, 'Sorry about that, by the way. It was stupid.' I nod and walk out.

When I get back I unlock the door using the spare key and go into the sitting room. Cress is crying. She's lying face down on some kind of portable bed-table. She has towels over her.

'Marlow, this is Ruth, Ruth this is Marlow – he's my brother.' Cress looks red-faced, tears falling down her cheeks.

'Ruth is just giving me a massage,' Cress sniffs.

'I thought she was doing your taxes,' I say. 'Why are you crying?'

'Bugger off and I'll tell you later,' she puts on a smile which isn't convincing. Ruth looks up, raises an eyebrow.

'Ruth, that's a nice name,' I say.

'It's a Biblical name,' she adds, with an ironic grin.

'Like David . . . or God?' I say.

'Sod *off*,' Cress laughs.

In the kitchen she has all kinds of things that I didn't

think models were supposed to have. Maybe she just bought them to impress me. I start cooking bacon and eggs and some sausages – they have sun-dried tomatoes in them, though – and the frying heats the room up so I take off my sweatshirt and open a window. I serve out the meal and put Cress's in the oven on a plate. I sit there and eat away by myself, read a magazine I just bought. After about ten minutes I hear the front door slam – Ruth leaving. Cress walks into the kitchen.

'That feels better,' she announces. I point to the oven. 'Oh, lovely. Cooked breakfast for me at eight in the evening,' she says sarcastically, taking it out of the oven.

'What are you looking at, brother?'

'I didn't think models ate.'

'Well I do. I do shitty soap ads, not catwalk.'

'So why were you crying? Was the queen of the Old Testament beating you up?'

'No, haven't you had a massage? Sometimes it makes you feel sad. It's normal.'

'Why does that happen?'

'I don't bloody know.'

'So you pay her to come over and make you cry. I could do that for free.' She laughs at that, and my throat immediately tightens. Maybe I'm torturing her with every moment I say nothing.

'These eggs are nice,' Cress says, chomping away. She chomps, it's sweet – who'd think a model would chomp? If you saw Cress you'd think she must be pleasant. She has that kind of beauty that says: 'you'll like me.' Peri has a kind of *you don't know what I'm thinking and you never will* slant to her eyes; she exudes the kind of hard beauty which looks like it came from being on the run.

Later, I'm sitting watching television and Cress comes in, towelling her hair dry. She sits down by me.

'Maybe it'll be okay, sharing a flat. We could get to know each other,' she says. 'It'll be a challenge. I'd like to meet the girls you like. I've never met any of your girlfriends.'

I don't say anything.

'What d'you do at weekends?' she asks.

'Friday I worked. Saturday I worked. Sunday I drew a picture which I threw away.'

'Work? So what happened to Lourdes?'

'Went to Lisbon?'

'Why?'

'She didn't say.'

'What was she like?'

'She was okay,' I say.

'Lucy went,' Cress says, giving up on that line of questioning. 'She was feeling better. You could have said something more. That's pretty amazing that Peri has come back. D'you know where she goes the whole time?'

'I've no idea where she goes.'

'Don't you think about her, ever?'

'No. I never think about her.'

Peri is probably sitting on my bed at this moment, rocking gently, tearing up paper into tiny pieces of confetti for no reason, drinking and drinking, not getting dressed all day. Sitting there. Just sitting there, ticking.

251

'You know, you just say those kinds of things. I don't believe you.' Cress says. 'D'you ever think about school? About all the things that went on?'

'Never.'

'That's weird,' she says. She takes the towel off her head.

'Jesus, you've gone super blonde,' I say.

'Yeah. What d'you think?'

'You look like you did when you were a little girl, before you were a home-renting young woman.'

'I am a little girl, *Marlow*,' she says, affecting a nasal tone, very close to her actual voice when she was a child. I feel my head tightening through lack of oxygen; I feel drowsy like drowning in neat, warm whisky.

'Where are you going?' she says, as I pull myself up and run into the bathroom. 'You all right?' she says.

'Yeah,' I manage, out of breath, my heart thumping. I fill a glass of water and sit on the side of the bath. The woman who stands in a fine spray of water, her eyes looking up at heaven, dressed in a bikini, was just a little girl in front of me. I come out of the bathroom.

'I've got to tell you something,' I say.

252

25.

AREN'T YOU GOING TO SAY ANYTHING?

Cress bounces in at 7.30 a.m. and wakes me up. I didn't tell her. I bottled out.

'I'm off on a job today,' she says. She switches the radio off. 'D'you always sleep with music on?' She picks up the phone and goes into the kitchen with it. I can hear her talking and then I fall back to sleep. I come round again to the sound of her mobile phone ringing. It's decorated with gold stars – the kind you get for making a wobbly plate in pottery class. Old tickets for concerts are on her wall, pictures of people she and I have known for ages. A picture of our parents looks down at me from above. I hate it when photos are put up high like that, so that they're looking down at me, judging me. I nearly have to turn it around to face the wall, but that would be too bad. You're only supposed to do that when someone's dead, aren't you? I can't concentrate on the television, there's something nagging at me and it's Peri's voice, screaming, *You must tell her, Marlow.*

I get out of bed, look out through the window. I look out over the well-heeled street. Old money is everywhere you look. Across the road is a pub which has an enclosed garden patio, protected by walls with climbing plants all over them. Plants and trees encase it – a magic garden in the city. The street is wide, and the sun finds its way into the flat with no difficulty. Someone passes, walking a dog. Even the dog looks like it has always had money. This gives me a false sense of safety. I have a shower; it's one of those power ones which buffs you to within an inch of your life. I come out renewed, get dressed, make a cup of tea. I flick the radio back on, and drink my tea. The doorbell goes. I open the door and a woman is standing there.

'Is Cress here?' she asks me.

'No, she's working today.'

'Oh, d'you know what?' she says, flicking her Fulham hair.

'What?'

'No, do you know what she's working on?'

'Who're you?'

'I'm dropping some photos round for her, from a shoot.' She hands me a portfolio. 'Bye then,' she says, frowning a little. She walks down the stairs. I stand there at the top of them with the portfolio in my hand. She looks back up once she's reached the bottom.

'She *does* live here, doesn't she?' she asks.

'Yes,' I say. The girl shakes her head as if she needs someone else there to agree with her, to say 'Yes, her brother isn't very friendly, is he?' She disappears. I take the portfolio inside, shut the door behind me, turn the radio up.

The doorbell goes again.

I get back up, this time like an old man. I *just* miss banging my head on the low door frame for the second time. When I open the door, there's a different woman, probably in her early twenties, looking at me. She looks pale and drawn, but her eyes are vivid, imaginative, livid green. She is sharp angles. I don't know if she's glaring at me or smiling at me. I stand aside and motion for her to come in. I want to say how great it is to see her, even though I saw her two or three days ago. I want to say how I've missed her, not just these last few days, but constantly and over so many years. I want to put my arms around her, and then tell her how I hate her. I hate her for putting pressure on me to screw up my sister. I never asked her to interfere. I want to ask her why the hell she's standing in the same room as me now, when I wish she wasn't, and when all I've wanted forever is for her to be in the same room.

'Aren't you going to say anything?' Peri stands in front of me. I can hear Cress's phone ring in the background. The answering machine clicks in and some woman says that she has a booking for next week. Peri sits down by me.

'I like the way Lucy thinks you *just* got back,' I say.

'Did she come round?'

'You know she came round.'

'Why is this taking so long?'

'Peri, have you seen what your pupils look like?'

'*Well* . . .' she says. 'Why is it taking so—'

'I've not said anything to Cress, if that's what you mean. And if you'd give me a few days I'm sure I can approach this, I'm sure there's a way I can tell her. I need to speak to my dad again.'

'What does your mum say?' she asks.

255

'Oh, I don't know. Mum and Dad are kind of living apart at the moment.'

Peri stands up, fixes me with her cold stare.

'I don't want to tell her, Peri,' I say. 'She's the happiest person I know. I think if she knew . . . y'know, I mean can you imagine . . .'

'Yes, I *can* imagine, Marlow. I can imagine perfectly. And what does *y'know* really mean? Eh? It means sexually assaulted.'

I put my hands over my ears.

'Oh, how sweet,' Peri says. 'What you don't hear won't hurt you, eh? That should be the motto for all our families. There's probably a thousand things in her life that she doesn't understand. There's a thousand things which she does and doesn't know why. And they're all down to this event. She earns her living showing off her body, for fuck's sake. I'm sure there's something in that.'

'You don't know what you're talking about. It's just speculation.'

'This is why she must know,' she shouts. She lights a cigarette. 'Do you even know the exact sequence of events?'

'No.'

'I would think about those strangers and her for a while. Think about them, locking the door . . . think about them—'

'I know what you're doing, Peri. You'll damage her.'

'She has to know.'

'You're not even family. Why is it any of your business?'

256

'You told me, I know her, I've known her for a long time.'

'But that doesn't give you the right.'

'I *am* part of this. I'm part of all of you now.'

And she keeps going and keeps going. She tells me that I shouldn't listen to my parents, to anyone except her. I have to change my sister's life.

'I just want longer to think about it.'

'I'm serious, Marlow. I can find her today, easily enough.'

'What d'you mean?'

'I can find her and tell her. By lunch-time she'll know.'

'You do that . . . it'd tear our family apart.'

'Sounds like it's not doing so well at the moment, anyway.'

'At least my parents aren't fucking drug addicts.'

'The lot of them should be locked up, they're all as bad—'

'They're not. We're not the same as you. Cress is not the same as you. She's in a much better way than you are.'

'Only because she doesn't fucking know.' Her voice, her face, are blurred to me. I can feel myself close in; I'm getting buffeted by her; I feel like I must close down, make myself invisible.

'So you'll tell her today,' she spits. I kind of nod in agreement. I'm sitting with my back hunched, my hands sweating as they hold my face. I feel myself getting smaller. I look at the ground.

'Marlow, either you say you'll do it today or I'll do it. Then we can get on with things.'

'What *things?*'

'Just things. You and me,' she shrugs. It seems fake. It seems she just made that up to tempt me, to manipulate me.

'I think you're unstable, Peri. You don't want me. You just want Cress as a companion in all of this.'

'Just do it, Marlow.'

Something in me triggers and I find myself standing in the middle of the room. Our speech speeds up.

'What're you doing?' she says.

'You won't tell her,' I say.

'I'm going to—' her speech is stopped as I push her against the wall. Her eyes narrow, but she doesn't look surprised. 'You think I'm scared, Marlow? I'm not scared of you.'

'Listen. I'm asking you, please . . .'

'God, you're pathetic,' she says.

'I'm *telling* you to leave her alone.' My grip on the base of her neck tightens. 'You'll leave her alone. Don't come back here, or to my flat.'

'I'm going to see my fucking idiot parents, anyway,' she spits. 'I thought I better re-introduce myself to them, see if they can remember me.'

'Cress has nothing to do with you or your sick experiments. Leave her alone.'

'It's your parents who are into the sick experiments. Me and your dear sister are just the result.'

'You aren't the result of anything. You never really spoke to her, so don't make out like you've always been friends, like there's some bond. They just tried to put two kids together who had been through similar

258

things. But you and her never talked, never recognised a similarity. *We* became friends, for fuck's sake. So don't pretend now that there's a cosmic bond between the two of you.'

I open the front door to the flat. She looks at the door and then at me. I reach for her and grab her arm and pull her out of the room. She reluctantly stumbles to the door.

'Aren't you going to hit me?' she asks.

'Get out!' I shout, my face inches away from hers.

'There'll be a time when you won't be able to protect her, just like you couldn't before.'

'You want a buddy for your club.'

She just looks at me.

'If you do, Peri,' I say.

'What?'

'If you do . . .' I say and slam the door.

26.

SLOWLY SLIP AWAY

I take the Tube up to North London. After a while you can see cows in fields as the train rushes along, clattering. In the British Newspaper Library, they make me do a test before I'm allowed to use the microfiche. This is particularly sick, as my heart is already pounding, thinking about what I'm looking for. After my lesson, the woman who showed me how to work the machine asks me what I'm looking for.

'Just old newspaper articles,' I say.

'Well, obviously,' she says. I wait for her to leave and go back to her desk. It take five hours to wade through the acres of fuzzy text on the screen: other people's history is of no interest to me today. Finally, I find a references to the incident in the Paradise Arcade. The incident with Peri. It mentions that it isn't the first of its kind, but gives no more details. Unusually, they publish a picture of one of them – perhaps it was before they withheld identities in case a lynch mob set out to kill them. Me. The man doesn't look anything like I thought. I always imagined him smart, maybe a jacket, trousers with a crease. He was scruffy, with old jeans, and his hair looked unkempt. He was unshaven and had a moustache. He wore a white T-shirt, dirty with age and ripped at the side, almost hanging off him. In the centre of the shirt was a picture in yellow and black. It was of a smiley face.

Peri thought about it for two days; two days when she turned herself inside out, drank and ate a year's prescription, fought with her parents. And then she decided it was time for another casualty, a companion. And when I walk in the door of Cress's flat, it feels like I watch Cress for hours. When I replay it in my mind, it seems as if there must have been hours and hours when Cress was sitting on the window ledge just looking into the air. She must have been sitting in the window, like a scared child on the top of a high diving board.

But the first thing I see as I look out the window is her, lying on her side on a lower part of the roof. I feel my neck tense, my eyes strain, I'm so scared. I never thought Peri would do it; I never thought she would do this to me. For what reason? I run to the window, put my hands on the ledge, steady myself – I nearly jump out after her. I look down below. There's a large gap, which I have to jump over. I don't know how the hell she got across there.

Down there, on the floor, Cress lies.

There's no movement in the air, no wind, no trees rustling, no movement in her body. I grab her mobile phone, which is sitting on the table by the window ledge, call the ambulance, then throw the phone back into the room. She moves a little.

'*Cress*,' there's a disgusting edge to my voice, it's when you wonder if that's the last time you might say a person's name actually *to* them.

'*Cress*,' I say, my tonsils and mouth swollen, not letting me speak. They catch on the back of my mouth, I choke. She turns her head slightly. I look back into the room, think about what I can use to get down there. The skin on my face feels red and angry, and I only realise now that I'm crying steadily, but my heartbeat is so strong I can't hear or feel anything else. I keep expecting to see a wicked-grinning Peri standing silently in the corner, pleased with her work. All there is of Peri, though, is her lighter on the table. I see nothing in the room I can use. I get out onto the ledge, stand up on it. Cress moves again. Her lip is bleeding. Hair covers the rest of her face, covered in sweat, sticking in fine strands to her skin.

'*OhmyGod*,' I say. Tears choke my speech into staccato fractions of words. Her body is absolutely still for a deadening moment. Then she moves again, extending her arm, reaching out, up into the air towards me – a pleading, begging hand. One of her eyes isn't even open, and pain is visible in the other one, its brightness dying against her child-blonde face. Her little hand reaches up to me, so many feet above her, so helpless. I reach my hand down, there's a distance between us, I can't breathe. If we could both extend our arms by fifteen feet, our hands would be touching.

I jump back into the room. Glued to my palm is one of the sticky gold stars that has come off her phone. I tear up the bed. The mattress, the duvet, the pillows all fly out of the window, like they're gasping for air. Feathers from the pillows escape into the stillness. They land a little way away from her. She's still looking up at me, silently.

263

I crouch as low as I can, my feet on the window ledge. I look down below once more, gauge the gap I have to jump. Then I do it, jump, spring into the air, my body slightly angled forward like an elevating helicopter. With every bit of muscle and bone and cartilage and gristle I have, I project myself with all my height, into the air and fly like a basketball player floating to the hoop. Explode. Elevate. Let go. Relax. Fall. The next thing I hear is the sound of my hands smacking onto the hard floor which sends a cracked pulse through the rest of my body as its fall is broken by the mattress. I stand up, move over to her. I put my face next to hers, our cheeks together. I can hear her breathing tiny, quick, frightened breaths. I put my hand in hers, but she doesn't grip it. I imagine a ladder appearing above the window, and paramedics descending like ants in an Escher picture, coming down from all angles with a pulley and rescue stretcher attached to the building.

'What did you do, what have you done?' I whisper to her. There are no marks on her clothes. 'Where did you jump from?'

An empty bottle of vodka rolls out from under her jacket towards me, the glass crackling over the rough, sandblasted roof surface.

'Jump?' she whispers back.

'Eh?' I pull my face away a little, put my arm around her, listen to her breath, will her not to stop.

'Drunk . . .' she says.

'You're drunk?' I say. She gives a little look that means she's agreeing with me. I look up behind me, look at the gap I jumped. To one side there's a thin fire escape ladder attached to the wall, just outside the bathroom. There is no gap there. She could have climbed down there and got onto the roof. And soon paramedics *will* come down that ladder and then they'll take her and they'll perform one of many routine, successful stomach pumps in London on a Tuesday evening.

The weeks and months that followed, plodded slowly past us all. I had the urge to keep in contact with everyone I ever met. Joel was now painting album covers and working at a small record label whose manifesto was to release records by bands who wouldn't find a voice elsewhere. Some would say there was a good reason for that. His band were no more. There was a big fight at one of their concerts and that was it. The fight was just between the band members.

Richie worked for a while in the video shop he used to mess around in. His impressions were the delight of the customers who came back and would rent films, knowing that he would take their money and wish them a good evening in the style of the actor or actress in the film. He quit that job, got an agent and did the stand-up circuit up and down the country. He loved it. I even saw him on television at three a.m. once, something about the Edinburgh Festival.

He started his routine with one-liners I remember him saying ten years earlier. Then he did something about how it was so hard to know what women wanted nowadays: 'You ask them round to your house, you do wheelies on your bike for half an hour in front of them, you take them up to the service station for chips, spend the rest of the evening on the gambling machines . . . and they never call you.' He got even more famous as there was always stuff in the papers about being politically correct – a new phrase that makes Americans feel less guilty for having ghettos with liquor stores and gun shops on every corner. It was a gift for Britain; we're as guilty. And we have a longer history. Richie would have enough material to take over the world one day.

Marty had become a junior motocross champion and then broke his leg badly. He recovered, but never competed again. His dad won a load of money on Ernie and bought a motorcycle shop which they ran together. That was beautiful. We hadn't spoken since the party at Simon's house, but we would send postcards quite often. Always just postcards. No strings.

And my sister. Time passed slowly for me as well, realising that whether I had got to Cress's house an hour earlier, or two days later, it would have made no difference. You can't protect a person from their life. You *cannot* do it. The image of her lying there when I arrived haunts me; I can't make it disappear – that initial thought that Cress had tried to kill herself. But she'd been drinking at home, while Peri was with her, and after Peri left. Then she felt hot because of the allergic reaction to the alcohol. She went into the bathroom, climbed outside, then passed out, lying on the roof. What was more difficult to work out was, if the outcome had been different, what would have happened to Peri. And the idea that Peri could be so cruel.

Later, I would think back to her family – the infidelity,

the fights and deals between parents, their indifference to their children – and wonder if she was just hell-bent on destroying ours as well. If Cress had killed herself because of Peri's perverse desire to share the experience with someone, what would have happened? In a way, that Cress did something as mild as she did: get drunk and position herself somewhere where she could be reached, was typical. The act of selfishness, of self-destruction, not to mention rashness, was not in her personality. And I'm sure there was a part in Peri that hated that, that wished Cress would dissolve and finally give up on fighting against a memory, like Peri did five days later, when she was found dead at a flat that she owed two months rent on.

If Cress *had* a sleeping memory of when she was assaulted, then Peri telling her would have awakened it. Because Peri remembered everything so clearly, she thought Cress would suddenly get a flashback and remember it all. But it didn't happen. The pure shock, maybe disbelief, as well as finding out that it was Peri who was also taken, was what caused her to drink. But maybe she stopped before it was too late, or maybe she was just lucky. The shock of hearing Peri's words – so incredible, why would she make it up? – well, how could anyone react to that? So my little sister decided to sit on the roof for a bit. And there are no answers to what will shape your life, only arguments going in different directions.

As I sat on the edge of the hospital bed, the stench of post-stomach pump still wretched in the air, I watched my parents stand together, in the same corner of the room, looking at their girl. My father put his arm around my mother and I felt him drawing the family in, bringing it together, gripping what he had helped create, what he had left. Not ever letting go. And they were still there, two days later, watching their girl recover, eating a bowl of apple sauce, lying in bed. After three days she left hospital, went to stay with my parents in the land of roundabouts. But it wasn't my father who helped Cress get through it, although he was there. It was my mother who spent days, weeks, months with her daughter. And it was over those months that, very slowly, her true personality crept back, as guilt gave way to compassion. It was over that time that I remembered what my mother used to be like, before the life was squeezed out of her by guilt for something she had no control over. The intensity between her and Cress built, and was what was needed to get past something like this. I just have one image in my head, of the two of them sitting down, talking, and how similar they actually looked: they were mother and daughter, but now more so than ever.

New Year's Day when I was thirteen or fourteen. Before any of this, before Dad knew he was going to leave my mother, only to return to her in a small hospital cubicle. Cress and I were walking around in the New Year's Day snow in the garden. It was so cold and we both had woolly hats on. Dad opened the window.

'Look at you two, those stupid hats,' he said, laughing. Cress did her newly-learnt V sign at him, and stuck her tongue out. He did it back and laughed. I looked at him. He was unshaven as usual; he was born unshaven.

'Let's go for a walk.' Cress said.

'Okay.'

We walked across the nearby fields, Cress leading the way.

'Where are we going?'

'Just for a walk. I always go this way.'

We kept plodding through the snow. The drifts were piled up by the fences and hedges. We walked up one drift which was so large that the view over it was blocked. We climbed up, our boots making that squeaking sound, the friction of rubber against snow. As we got to the top of the drift a view of the small valley below opened up in front of us. There was an enormous area of concrete with bits of rubble scattered around it. And a building, holding on for dear life. Concrete cancer, as Dad called it.

'Look at that,' I said.

We stared at the remains of the arcade. It had been eaten alive by some weird disease. So they tried to blow it up. Which didn't work. We had a leaflet through the door saying to close the windows because of the dust. But there was no dust, and barely an explosion. It still stood there, mostly intact. I remember Dad telling me a year later about how sometimes, a man dies and then a few weeks later his wife of sixty years dies as well. He thought maybe the building wanted to die, so it brought the cancer on itself. Cress walked along, swinging her arms. Her bobble hat jigged about as she navigated the snow.

'I'm going back. I'm cold,' I said.

She didn't listen to me and carried on walking. I gave in and followed her down to the car park by the arcade, found a concrete girder to sit on. Work vehicles were parked, stagnant over the holiday period, frozen yellow dinosaurs. They wanted to turn the car park into something. Most projects started, but ran out of money. Just like the council ran out of explosives in the first place. Cress wrapped the scarf around her face. She sat there, her arms hugged around her body. I blew onto my freezing hands.

'This concrete is making my arse freeze,' I said. I looked up and saw a dot on the snowdrift horizon. 'Who the hell is that, coming down here?'

'Peri.'

'Eh?'

'That's Peri.'

'That dot is Peri?'

The dot got larger; it became a female form. Peri was moving towards us, picking her steps in the snow. Cress looked out over the snow. Her eyes caught Peri's as she got closer. Peri suited the snow. She looked like she could walk the landscape for days and always look the same. Cress got up, walked up to her. I stood up, my backside numb with cold. Both girls looked at me.

'It's so cold,' I said.

I walked towards Peri. Under her hat and scarf her eyes gleamed, cut through the freezing air, to me.

'Shall we go back to the house?' The two girls nodded at the idea. We climbed slowly up the hill, our boots slipping from time to time. As we got to the top I took a step and my foot disappeared under me. I fell forwards and suddenly I was up to my waist in snow. I could feel nothing below me, I could waggle my feet freely. I looked down. I was in a deep hole in the snowdrift. My arms were outstretched on firm surface-level snow, which was keeping me from falling. The girls looked round. Peri knelt down, then lay on her stomach, put her arms out. Cress held onto Peri's legs to stop her slipping. My hands found Peri's. Some snow fell away where the pressure of my body was pushing it. I slipped a little further. If Peri let go, my entire body would be below the line of the snow drift. Peri was silent, her hands holding mine like a vice, clasped around mine so tightly that if I fell she would fall with me. Her grip on me was like a gecko, like my old lizard when it got something in its mouth. It's not that it didn't want to let go; it just didn't know how to. And when it gripped something it held on to it until it died. Cress dug her heels in and pulled on Peri's legs, like some reverse wheelbarrow race. Then Peri got to her knees and walked backwards on them with Cress holding on to her by her jacket. Bit by bit I came out of the hole, born again with ice melting and soaking me. I got to my knees. Peri's hand was bleeding. I looked down at where I had fallen – the drop was fifteen feet to the ground. A piece of barbed wire from the fence was sticking out where Peri had been lying.

'You're bleeding,' I said. She looked at her hand, the blood diluted by the melted snow. I held her hand as we walked back. She said it felt better like that, even though the cut was open. *Don't know how to let go.*

271

27.

A CHRISTMAS CAROL

It had been a hot summer. Despite my support Goran Ivanisevic lost in the final again. 'I feel like I am to die,' he said afterwards. We all did. People had started talking about the end of the century, the end of the millennium. We still had over a year to go. What else was there to say about it?

It was a cold winter, and despite my shouting at the television, bombs still dropped on people who must be getting used to us by now. There was a strange atmosphere during that week, the lead-up to Ramadan, the lead-up to Christmas, the lead-up to impeachment. And as various Western leaders whom I've grown up with either die, or wither beyond recognition, the ones whom we've bombed continue, stronger than ever, in my adulthood as they did in my childhood.

There's one woman, or maybe a couple, in most men's lives, who comes along and erases all the women who came before her, and probably taints all the women that may come after. She becomes a standard, but with no actual, measurable qualities – just something about her. With one look, with one kiss, with one fuck, she removes all those old lost loves who you thought you might bump into one day. She tears through your life, modernising you, changing you, making you look forwards instead of

273

backwards, making you fall for her. She's always there. The woman I can smell on me now, whose tapes litter this car, has taken Peri – someone she's never met – and started pushing her into the background.

I phone from a hands-free mobile and hear my mother's voice. I chew the cord while I talk.

'Oh, God, Marlow, is everything all right? Is anyone hurt?'

'No one's hurt? Why would anyone be hurt? I'm just going to be a bit late.'

'That's okay. Your father's still at the airport. The flight is delayed.'

'Well, I'll be there in an hour.'

'See you then, love,' she says. I nearly crash when she says love. I still can't get used to it. I'm the last person in the world to learn to drive, and the journey from London to the buckle of the commuter belt is slow. Holiday traffic. As I approach my parents house, I can see Dad's car there. He's arrived back before me. There's something comforting about his car being at the house. There's something comforting in them being back together, especially as it seems to be real. I pull up behind his car, switch the engine off.

Mum answers the door. I can see Dad in the background, trying to light the candles on the table, shaking the lighter which isn't working. The table has been beautifully decorated, the Christmas tree's warm lights glow. Dad gives up trying to light the candles, turns round, walks towards me. We shake hands. He smiles at me. A door slams upstairs, and I can hear footsteps

274

as someone descends. I look up as my sister makes her entrance. She bounces down the stairs, throws her arms around me.

'How is Miss New York?'

'She's fine. And have you broken my flat?' Cress says.

'No, it's in good order.'

'I've noticed your rent cheques going into my account quite regularly as well. I was shocked.'

She pulls away and smiles.

'Well, it's ready,' my mother says and walks into the kitchen. 'Let's eat.'

'Oh, Marlow, there's some post for you somewhere,' Dad says. He lifts up a pile of magazines with celebrities dressed up as Santa Claus on the front. A couple are bank statements, there's also a letter and a postcard. I look at the back of the card: just my first name, spelt wrongly, and an attempt at the address. On the other side is a scrawl which I bring closer to my eyes to try to make out. 'Marley's Ghost. Marley was dead to begin with. There is no doubt whatever about that.' It continues, getting messier as it flows down the page. Dad sees me looking at it, puzzled. I hand it to him.

'That's *A Christmas Carol*. The very beginning,' he says. I take another look at it.

'I love that book,' Mum says.

'What's on the other postcard?' Dad asks.

'I didn't see another postcard.'

'Oh, it must be under some papers. I'm sure there was another one,' he says. I watch Mum move around the kitchen. She tries to pull a tray of roast potatoes out of the oven but can't grip with the tea towel. I watch as Dad puts his hands over hers and they hold it, half each, and take it out.

'This is great,' I say, as we start eating.

'Yes, it is,' Mum says. Dad smiles. He's watching in amazement as Cress puts a huge piece of turkey in her mouth. He's moving his head, as if to help her chew it. He can't take his eyes off her. There's the smallest area of discoloration on her top lip – a small scar which, unless you knew her before, you'd never notice. She looks healed. Everyone in this room looks healed in some way.

'This is nice,' Mum sighs. Just in general.

When lunch is finished we sit in the other room and a few people come round. Donald still wanders about, practising his golf swing with an invisible club. Cress is the golden girl – everyone wants to know about the girl who attends the dance academy in New York. She answers questions in between calling her boyfriend in America. Mum keeps referring to him like she knows him; it's quite endearing.

'I should think Michael would love this,' Mum says, as if she knows everything about him. Quite what the 'this' is that she's referring to, we don't know.

'When is he arriving, again?' Mum says.

'New Year's Day,' Cress says. 'I've told you a hundred times. But don't put on anything fancy, okay?'

'Must be just like *Fame*,' Heather Mottishead says, enthusiastically.

'What?' Cress asks.

'Your dance academy . . . in New York.'

'Well, actually it's not . . .' I watch Cress's face change and give in, like she's answered the same question a million times. 'Yes, I suppose it is,' she relents, kindly.

'It's all very exciting, isn't it, Marlow?'

'I'm very excited,' I say. Cress punches me on the arm. Heather goes and bothers someone else.

My mother comes up to me an hour later. She's still holding a tray of sherry and mince pies.

'If you want to go out for a bit, that's fine. You've done your duty. And you,' she says to Cress, 'You needn't hang around with us oldies.' It's something my mother has never said before. Over in the corner Dad has broken away from the chatter. He's looking out the window. I walk up to him.

'Everything all right, Marlow?' he says, cheerily.

'Actually it is.'

'How's work?'

'It's fine. It's hard work on newspapers, isn't it? They want their photos the same day.'

'Bloody newspapers,' he says. He smiles. 'I hear you have a reason not to work so late.'

'Uh huh.'

'What does she do?'

'She's an osteopath,' I say. 'She makes people taller.'

'Does she unbend you after games?' He gives me a stupid look.

'She does. She's even learnt the rules. Afterwards, she tells me who should've got fouls for illegal defence, and where I should have layed up instead of dunked. Got a big game next week.'

277

'Why don't you bring her over in the New Year?' he says. Cress comes up to me and hands me a postcard, the one that was lost. I stuff it in my pocket.

'It's great to see you and Mum happy again,' I say.

'If you start forgiving early enough, you can sometimes finish before the end of your lifetime,' Dad says. 'When someone hurts you, start forgiving them the same day. That way you both might only be a few years older when you can talk again. And you won't have wasted a bitter lifetime.'

I take a glass of punch. It's warm and smells of spices and hot, burnt oranges. Little Christingle oranges decorate the fruit bowl, all the effort that my mother put in, all the effort it takes. I watch Cress pick one up, hold it in front of her like a crystal ball. She frowns, trying to remember when she last held one. I remember. I remember everything. But I'm about to start forgetting. I'm about to start forgetting whole warehouse's of things. Don interrupts Cress to tell her about the new course which has been developed on the arcade site. He's talking about how yesterday his golf opponent cheated.

'Really?' Cress says, sounding bored.

'Yes. We were on the seventeenth and he miraculously "found" his ball right in the semi-rough, when he'd hooked it miles right.'

'That's terrible,' Cress says, 'What a . . .' she looks round, '. . . bastard.' She looks back at Don. 'Sorry, Donald,' she says, and looks over at me, I hold her gaze, and then I look away, move away. As Mum walks past Dad, her wedding ring tarnished with age, she stops, bends down and kisses him. All around us, people are talking, there's a faint hum from a radio on somewhere. I look at Lourdes's postcard. The postmark is Lisbon. Cress pulls herself away from Don.

'Who was the letter from?'

'Lourdes.

'No, I mean the letter,' she says, seriously. I pull the bank statement and the letter out of my back pocket, hand it to her. The front of it has got wet, and it has re-direction stickers all over it. The postman's scribbles of possible postcodes are scratched all over it. It was posted a long time ago.

'Recognise this writing?' she says. I study it for a second.

'Oh, God. Yes, I do.'

'May I?' Cress says. I nod. She walks slowly over to the fireplace, looks over to me once, and then cremates the last bit of Peri in the flames.

I walk outside to read part two of Lourdes' Christmas message. The air is cold and fresh, the sun breaking through a little, and the light makes the silver writing sparkle.

'He became as good a friend, as good a master, and as good a man, as the good old city he knew, or any other good old city, town, or borough, in the good old world. Some people laughed to see the alteration in him, but he let them laugh, and little heeded them; for he was wise enough to know that nothing ever happened on this globe, for good, at which some people did not have their fill of laughter in the outset . . . His own heart laughed; and that was quite enough for him.'

I stuff the postcard in my pocket.

'Are you coming back in?' Cress says, hanging in the doorway.

'No. No, I'm not.'